They're wanted . . . in the worst possible way.

"If anyone sees these three young women, please contact the FBI immediately," the newscaster finished. "Once again, they are considered armed and dangerous." The plastic-looking anchor paused. "Alarmingly, that hasn't stopped teenage girls all over the country from taking up the cause of this mysterious Terrorist Trio. Parents are concerned."

Jo, Caylin, and Theresa stared at one another over the plates of rapidly cooling breakfast. None of them had taken so much as a bite of their meals.

"We're a *cause?*" Caylin asked softly. "What does that *mean?*"

"I think I'd laugh if our butts weren't on the line," Jo whispered.

"We're like a cartoon," Theresa agreed. "Or a bad afternoon sitcom."

"Whoa . . . check this out." Jo turned back to the television.

"The women in the Terrorist Trio, are, like, conspiracy victims," one of the girls, made up like Caylin, told a reporter. "The system is against us! Young women get *no* respect!"

Suddenly Caylin swiveled around to face the TV set. "You go, sister!" she burst out. "Right on!"

Jo cringed as every person in Moody's Diner turned to stare at their table.

Don't miss any books in this thrilling new series:

#1 License to Thrill
#2 Live and Let Spy
#3 Nobody Does It Better
#4 Spy Girls Are Forever
#5 Dial "V" for Vengeance *
#6 If Looks Could Kill *

Available from ARCHWAY Paperbacks

* Coming soon

Nobody Does It Better

by

Elizabeth Cage

AN ARCHWAY PAPERBACK
Published by POCKET BOOKS
New York London Toronto Sydney Tokyo Singapore

AN ARCHWAY PAPERBACK *Original*

An Archway Paperback published by
POCKET BOOKS, a division of Simon & Schuster Inc.
1230 Avenue of the Americas, New York, NY 10020

Spy Girls™ is a trademark of Daniel Weiss Associates, Inc.

Produced by 17th Street Productions,
a division of Daniel Weiss Associates, Inc.
33 West 17th Street, New York, NY 10011

ISBN: 0-671-02288-1

First Archway Paperback printing January 1999

10 9 8 7 6 5 4 3 2 1

Printed in the U.S.A.

IL 7+

To Dan and Jessica—congratulations

Nobody Does It Better

Josefina Mercedes Carreras—called "Jo" by anyone who wanted to continue life unhampered by a swift kick in the butt—strode down the tarmac of the Seattle-Tacoma airport Sunday night. The 747 express from the Czech Republic to New York had been a nightmare. The flight attendant had run out of peanuts, Jo's book had been about as interesting as one of those complimentary airline catalogs, and the two movies shown had been *Return of the Beach Nuts* and *My Invisible Stepmom.* Gag! Unfortunately the second leg of the journey—a direct flight from New York to Seattle—had been only marginally better. There had been peanuts aplenty.

"Can anyone say, 'java'?" Jo asked as she gazed around the nearly empty airport in search of a coffee bar. "I think I feel a major case of jet lag coming on."

Caylin Pike set down her Louis Vuitton suitcase and tucked an errant strand of blond hair back under the black cowboy hat she was wearing. "Maybe we'll have an espresso machine at home base," she mused. "We *are* in the coffee capital of the world."

"Can we discuss decafs, cafs, and lattes later?" Theresa Hearth asked, peering over the large mirrored sunglasses she had put on before deplaning. "If I don't get into a shower and wash off this airplane grime pronto, I'm going to be labeled toxic by the U.S. government."

Jo nodded. Theresa was right, as usual. Now that she and her compatriots had landed in Seattle, downtime was *finito.* Uncle Sam would want them to get to headquarters, figure out their latest mission, and study any pertinent information—all before taking a moment for even a quick bathroom break.

And when Uncle Sam spoke, the girls listened. He was *el jefe más grande* at The Tower—plus he was their own private fearless leader, the man who had brought the trio together. Uncle Sam had guided the Spy Girls through their previous two missions, always offering words of encouragement. Ever mysterious—the guy's face seemed to be permanently obscured by smoke and mirrors—Uncle Sam held the girls' lives in his hands, usually via satellite. But Jo had mastered the difficult art of letting someone else call the shots. As a Tower agent she had learned that such sacrifices were often necessary. Ergo, she'd have to put her craving for a café mocha on pause.

"Duty calls," Theresa agreed. "Let's just hope this mish is calmer than the *last* one."

"I'll second that emotion," Jo said. "I've encountered enough Eastern European terrorists to satisfy my excitement quotient for a lifetime."

"Not I," Caylin declared. "Nothing is more appealing to me than kicking a bad guy from here to you-know-where."

"We know, Cay," Theresa drawled as Jo reached over and tugged on the brim of Caylin's cowboy hat.

Sometimes it was hard to believe that Jo, Caylin, and Theresa had known one another for only a few months. Sure, Jo had expected to make new friends when she'd been accepted to what she had *thought* was an elite East Coast college. Ha! College had turned out to be a top secret spy academy for which all three young women had been handpicked by the United States government. Jo, Caylin, and Theresa had been put through the most intense weeks of their teenage lives as they learned to work together to triumph over whatever evil of the week was threatening international security. Now they were like sisters . . . no, they were closer than sisters. The girls were practically conjoined triplets.

Smiling, Jo continued toward the baggage claim area. Uncle Sam had said they would find three limos waiting to whisk them individually to their local headquarters. At the relatively tender age of eighteen, Jo couldn't believe she had already become accustomed to limousines, disguises, and high-tech gadgetry. James Bond and Austin Powers had nothing on Jo Carreras. Or Caylin Pike. Or Theresa Hearth. The Spy Girls.

"Does my scarf look okay?" Theresa asked. "I

feel like I've got an *I Dream of Jeannie* thing goin' on."

Jo glanced at the hot pink scarf draped over half of Theresa's face and raised her eyebrows. "You do look a bit funky—but hey, this is Seattle. Anything goes."

Jo flipped her own scarf—long, black, gauzy, *très* cool—around the bottom half of her face. In her humble opinion the scarves were a bit over the top. But Uncle Sam had insisted the girls use at least minimal disguises and split up *pronto* when they hit the States. Apparently grunge locals couldn't be trusted.

The trio stopped in front of the double automatic doors under a ground transportation sign. Theresa skimmed the small note card that copilot George Watson had handed her as she stepped off the plane. "I get the white limo," she read. "Caylin is in the gray, and Jo has black to go with her scarf."

"Blah, blah, blah, rules and regulations," Caylin moaned. "I feel like I should be saying something like, 'Roger, little bird, Shaun Cassidy has hit number one with 'Da Doo Run Run.'"

"What?" Theresa asked. She was tearing the note card into mote-size pieces.

Jo grinned. "Are you suggesting we break ranks?" she asked Caylin.

Caylin smiled back. "We could all use a little fun after that dismal plane ride . . . and what harm could a limo switcheroo *really* do?"

"None at all," Jo declared. In lieu of a caffeine

jolt she would have to settle for some old-fashioned Spy Girl fun.

As one, Uncle Sam's angels stepped forward. The electronic doors whooshed open and Jo breathed in the cool, damp northwestern air. At the side of the curb stood three limo drivers. Man in Gray. Man in White. Man in Black. How cute.

Jo didn't hesitate. She walked straight toward Mr. Gray—light brown hair, great build, hundred-megawatt smile. What more could she ask for when the rubber hit the road?

"Why am I not surprised?" Caylin mused aloud as she headed toward Mr. White, who, Jo noticed, looked about as friendly as a python.

"Ta ta!" Jo shouted. She brushed past the very hunky Mr. Gray and slipped into the plush backseat of the limo.

"Keep all hands and feet inside the vehicle!" Theresa called as she climbed into the black stretch ride parked at the head of the line.

Jo settled against the soft leather seat and closed her eyes. She half expected a laser light show to begin, the doors to lock, and Uncle Sam's shadowed face to appear on some kind of hidden TV screen. But there was only silence. Aha! The mission wasn't so pressing that The Tower felt the immediate dispatch of instructions was required. Good. With a bit of luck and a lot of Spy Girl style, this mission would proceed as smoothly as it had begun.

Of course, until the girls received detailed instructions from The Tower, they wouldn't know what they were facing. Jo knew that Theresa, girl-hacker extraordinaire, was hoping the mission would be computer based. Boring! Jo concluded. She prayed for some kicks before she started drowning in bytes and hard drives.

A few minutes later Jo leaned forward and glanced at the chauffeur's license attached to the driver's-side visor. "So where are we going . . . Travis O'Rourke?" she asked, inserting her patented don't-you-want-to-look-at-a-beautiful-girl-in-the-rearview-mirror-when-she's-talking-to-you lilt. Gazing out of the smoky glass window, she saw that they were speeding up a seaside highway, the Pacific Ocean so close that she could almost feel its cold, salty water.

"To 902 Stratford Road," Travis answered, pointing eastward. "We've still got a ways to go."

Good, cute-boy, Jo answered silently. Now she'd have even more time to entice him with her Spy Girl wiles. Yes, this was going to be a very pleasant journey—and one that would hopefully result in a date for dinner and a movie. Something starring Meg Ryan or Tom Hanks, preferably. Jo was in the mood for romance. . . .

"So where's a good place to—" Jo stopped speaking midsentence. One of her Spy Girl sensors had just been sounded.

Yep. There it was again. A distinct squealing of tires.

Jo pressed the button of the power window, waiting impatiently for the smoked glass to disappear into the door frame. Faster. Come on. Faster. At last the window was down. Jo poked her head out of the limo window. "What the . . . ?"

The white limo carrying Caylin was no longer heading east. The chauffeur had driven across the highway partition and was now racing west, toward the ocean.

This was bad. Jo had to follow. Fast.

"Turn the limo around and follow that car!" Jo screamed at Travis. "Step on it!"

Travis glanced at her in the rearview mirror. "I'm sorry, miss, but I can't do that. My boss would fire me if I didn't follow orders."

Aahhh. There was nothing more annoying than a man who was cowed by authority. Luckily Jo didn't have that problem at the moment. Which meant she needed a plan B. In two seconds Jo processed the situation and settled on a plan of action.

She unzipped the oversize bag she had carried on the airplane and groped through the contents until she found what she was looking for. Aha! There it was. The small, travel-size hair dryer she had laid down plastic for at the duty-free shop in the Czech Republic.

Sorry, Trav. Nothing personal.

She stuck the nozzle of the hair dryer against the back of the driver's head, grateful that he hadn't raised the privacy shield. "Pull over the limo and get out," she ordered. "I'm taking the wheel."

"What?" Travis's voice was high and thin.

"Pull over and get out. I'm driving." She nudged

his head with the hair dryer. "Unless you want me to do something we'll both regret."

With a little more than a squeak, Travis slammed on the brakes. He had opened the door and tumbled out before the limo came to a complete stop.

Jo didn't waste any time. She climbed over the barrier between her and the front of the vehicle and slid into the driver's seat.

"I'm on my way, Cay!" Jo pressed the pedal to the metal and the limo surged forward. She would overtake Theresa's limo, grab herself some Spy Girl backup, and pursue.

The adventure had begun.

Scream? Cry? Laugh hysterically and assume she was on *Candid Camera*? Caylin couldn't decide on the appropriate response to the fact that her limo driver had just swung wildly off course.

Okay. Deep breath. Instinct told her to stay calm. Panicking would only make things—whatever *things* were—worse.

"Excuse me?" Caylin tapped semipolitely on the window that separated herself from the driver. "Where are we going?" Even if her driver couldn't hear her voice, Caylin was sure that he would notice that she was knocking on the glass.

The window lowered a couple of inches. "You probably want to know where we're going, huh?"

Caylin relaxed. The guy's voice was warm and friendly. "Yes . . . I mean, a second ago we were driving in the opposite direction."

The driver glanced at Caylin in the rearview mirror. Uh-oh. His eyes told a different story. They were dark, hard, and mean. "You'll see *exactly* where we're headed soon enough, compu-queen," he responded.

Yikes. This was trouble. Big trouble. Mr. Driver obviously thought that Caylin was Theresa. Anyone who knew anything about the Spy Girls knew that Theresa was Master of All Hackers. Or more accurately, Mistress of All Hackers. Which meant that the guy did, in fact, know something about the Spy Girls. And he knew that Theresa had been originally assigned to the white limo.

Oh, man. Something was seriously awry. Caylin had to get out of this particular moving vehicle ASAP.

She dove for the door handle.

Click. Click.

Caylin's heart sank even further into her toes as she recognized the sound of power locks. A moment later the privacy screen closed again. She was trapped!

"Great. Perfect. Wonderful. Splendiferous way to begin my stay in the great Northwest . . . ," Caylin mumbled to herself. She scooted to the back of the limo and pressed her face against the rear windshield.

In the distance there were headlights. Could it be . . . ?

"Please. Please, let those beacons in the night belong to Jo or T.," Caylin whispered.

Seconds later the headlights were closer. And then closer.

Caylin squinted. Yes! Jo was behind the wheel . . . and Theresa was by her side! And they were in hot pursuit of the white limousine. Things were definitely looking up. Jo and Theresa would save her.

Caylin shimmied back toward the driver's seat, pulled off her cowboy hat, and whipped off the huge Jackie O.-style sunglasses that had hidden most of her face. Disguise seemed pretty useless at this point.

"Hey, driver!" Caylin yelled, banging on the glass. "You are messin' with the wrong *chiquita!*"

He glanced at her again in the rearview mirror, his eyes amused.

"I'm serious!" Caylin yelled. "I've got friends in high places, buddy. And once they catch up with this overpriced hunk of metal, you're gonna be *history!*"

Adrenaline surged through Caylin's veins as she waited for Jo to come to the rescue. Stay focused, Pike, Caylin ordered herself. She had to think like a super-duper Spy Girl.

Description. She would need to give Uncle Sam a description of this guy.

Caylin leaned forward to get a better look at the driver. Black hair, dark eyes, major five o'clock shadow. He was attractive, but in a kind of ice-cold Ted Bundy serial killer way. Unfortunately the driver was cackling to himself, unconcerned by Caylin's warning of the fate that awaited him when her fellow SGs got ahold of him.

Caylin's eyes widened in horror as Captain Ice gripped the steering wheel and yanked it to the left. She noticed three things instantly.

One: The car was now hurtling down a very long wooden pier.

Two: There was a small tattoo of a rosebud on the back of Ice's neck.

Three: The limo was *still* hurtling down what was becoming a shorter and shorter pier.

Now, Jo. Now, T. I need you guys *now,* Caylin silently begged. She squeezed her eyes shut, repeating the mantra over and over. If they didn't hurry up *ahora,* they weren't going to be able to teach Rosebud a lesson in re: absconding with young maidens. Instead Caylin would be taking a long swim in some very cold water.

Seventy. Eighty. Ninety. Jo had watched the speedometer climb higher and higher as she struggled to overtake the white limo in front of her.

Picking up Theresa had been a cinch compared to this. Theresa's limo driver had been all too happy to relinquish his last passenger of the evening. If he had wondered about Jo's sudden appearance behind the wheel, he had kept it to himself.

Now Jo slammed on the brakes. The car fishtailed as she took a sharp left onto the pier.

"Careful!" Theresa cautioned, gripping the dashboard with both hands.

Jo forced herself to ignore the murky black water that lay on either side of the pier. One wrong move, one ill-advised tap on the steering wheel, and they'd both be shark bait.

Her eyes glued to the wooden slats of the pier, Jo pursued the white limousine. And then it stopped.

Jo screamed and stomped on the brake pedal. The gray limo screeched to a halt amid a terrifying squeal of tires.

"Omigosh!" Jo flung off her seat belt with a quick, practiced flick of the wrist. She threw the vehicle into park and opened the driver's-side door. A second later she was sprinting toward the white limousine—the back of which seemed to be bobbing up and down, resembling one end of a gigantic teeter-totter.

"Man. Oh, man. Oh, man." Jo tried not to go into full panic mode as she realized that the front half of the white limo was hanging off the pier. Jo reached the side of the white car and tugged on the left rear passenger door handle. Nothing. The automatic door locks were malfunctioning. Caylin was trapped inside.

Caylin yelled and kicked at the windows. Unfortunately the soft sole of Caylin's espadrille was no match for thick, bulletproof glass. Jo was also aware that the driver was also trying to force his way out of the car. She put his cries out of her mind and zeroed in on Caylin's frightened face. She had to help her friend. Immediately, if not sooner.

"What do we do?" Theresa yelled.

"I don't know," Jo responded. "Got any ideas?"

"We need a torch," Theresa stated. "We've got to get the glass to give way."

Jo didn't need to be told twice. She ran back to the gray limo and pulled a can of aerosol hair spray from her oversize canvas carry-on bag. She raced to Theresa's side and popped the top.

As Jo pressed the button on the top of the can, Theresa lit match after match from a pack the Spy Girls had picked up during their last dinner out in Prague. "Insta-torch!" Jo shouted, aiming the line of fire straight onto the back passenger-side window. Finally the heat of the makeshift torch caused the glass to crack.

Caylin kicked out the window and poked her head into the fresh air. "Heeelp!" she yelled.

Jo and Theresa dropped their tools and grabbed Caylin's arms. Seconds later she was free. The three girls stood on the pier, staring at one another for a long moment.

"What about . . . ?" Theresa pointed at the limousine.

"Yikes," Jo whispered.

Caylin's exit from the vehicle had caused the weight of the limousine to shift. The rear end of the long vehicle was inching upward to an impossible angle.

Theresa gasped. "It's going . . ."

"Straight into the ocean," Caylin finished.

As the girls stared in disbelief the elegant white car slid off the pier and into the Pacific Ocean.

"He's gone," Caylin whispered as the rear of the limo disappeared into the black water.

Jo stared at the expanse of ocean. There was nothing but waves. The evil driver and all of Caylin's bags had just ceased to exist. And there was nothing the Spy Girls could do but shiver in the cold night air and try to be psyched that they were all still alive.

What a night," Theresa said, sighing. "So much for the Seattle mish going smooth as butter."

"I almost died tonight," Caylin whispered for about the hundredth time in the last forty-five minutes.

In the backseat of the gray limo Theresa put her arm around Caylin's shoulders and squeezed. "We wouldn't have let that happen, Caylin."

"Yeah," Jo called from the front seat. "You're our only blond. We need you."

Caylin giggled. "I'm surprised my hair didn't just turn white. I've never been so petrified in my life."

"Here we are," Jo said, pulling the car up to the curb of a very dark street. "This is 902 Stratford Road. Just as my pal Travis told me."

"Our home away from home," Theresa said. "Or in this case, our headquarters away from headquarters."

Theresa peered out the limousine window to get a look at their latest digs. Huh. The shuttered storefront wasn't exactly as promising as the circle drive of the Ritz Hotel in London had been. Valet parking was out of the question.

The girls piled out of the limo. Theresa and Jo grabbed their bags and suitcases while Caylin shuddered, luggage-less, on the curb.

"You can borrow my clothes until you get new stuff," Theresa assured Caylin as Jo slid their Tower-issued key into the dead bolt lock at 902 Stratford Road.

Caylin stuck out her tongue. "Gee, how thrilling. I've always wanted to spend my days wearing a succession of outfits consisting of khakis and white button-down shirts."

Theresa snorted. "You're exaggerating." Caylin and Jo always teased Theresa mercilessly about the fact that she was fashion challenged—especially because Theresa's mom was a famous designer.

Jo opened the storefront door, and the girls walked in.

"Wow," Caylin said. "I guess this is what real estate agents refer to as a fixer-upper."

Theresa nodded. The room was dark, with high ceilings and a cold cement floor. Dusty tarps covered everything. There wasn't a thick fluffy carpet or velvet-upholstered settee in sight. "Well, at least we're safe," she allowed.

"I guess we all know what we have to do," Jo said, locking the door behind them.

"Call Uncle Sam," Theresa and Caylin chorused.

"And looky there . . . a speakerphone." Jo headed for the phone that was placed conspicuously on top of one of the larger pieces of tarp.

"They might not give us gold bathtubs or bidets," Theresa observed. "But you can always count on the good ole Tower to provide a form of immediate communication."

"I guess we're going to have to tell Uncle Sam about the limousine switcheroo." Jo groaned. "But I don't think he's going to appreciate our fun and games."

"I'll make the dreaded call," Caylin offered. "Considering you guys saved my life tonight, it's the least I can do."

"Payment enough for me," Jo said, backing away from the telephone.

Caylin punched in Uncle Sam's top secret direct number. They all looked at one another expectantly as the phone's ring blared out of the speakerphone.

"Girls?" Uncle Sam questioned the moment he picked up. "You're late."

"No shinola," Jo whispered, nudging Theresa.

"We, uh, had a little problem," Caylin answered. "It's really kind of funny . . . well, maybe *funny* isn't the right word. Um . . . one of the limo drivers might be dead."

Theresa nervously clenched and unclenched her fists. There was no point in beating around the proverbial bush. On the other end of the line Uncle Sam sighed deeply. As always, Theresa tried to discern something about the identity of their mysterious boss by listening to the sound of his voice. But all she could envision were shadows and fog.

"You better start from the beginning," Uncle Sam said. "And don't leave out any of the gory details."

Theresa and Jo gave Caylin encouraging pats on the back as she related the events of the past hour and a half to Uncle Sam. His silence throughout spoke volumes.

"And then we drove here," Caylin finished. "Minus my bags . . . and one driver."

For a long moment Uncle Sam didn't say anything. "Jo, get rid of the gray limo, and I mean *yesterday*," he said finally, speaking rapid-fire. "Wipe away all fingerprints and *any* trace that you were ever inside the vehicle."

"Check," Jo responded.

"Theresa and Caylin, prepare headquarters. I want you all ready to work first thing tomorrow morning." He paused. "If local law enforcement gets a sniff of tonight's events, we could have big, big trouble."

"Check," Theresa answered.

"And I need a description of the driver," Uncle Sam demanded. "I'll run a check on him and see if we can piece together an ID."

Caylin's face seemed to pale in the dim light as she recounted what details she could about the man who had tried to take her for a long drive off a short pier. "And he had a tattoo of a rosebud on the back of his neck," she concluded. "A small red rosebud."

She shuddered. "Who wants a tattoo on the back of his neck? Yuck!"

"We'll find out who," Uncle Sam answered. "Hopefully."

"Uh, sorry about the mishap," Caylin said. "We didn't mean to dump the limo driver into the ocean—honest."

"Let's just hope that the mission proves easy enough to get you out of town before the you-know-what hits the fan," Uncle Sam answered darkly. "Cleaning up this mess is going to take all of my resources. I'll have to go to the highest levels of authority. I don't think you want to know just *how* high."

"Is that all, boss?" Jo asked. "I want to get to that limo before the sun rises."

"That's all—for now," he responded. "I'll give out the details of your mission when Jo returns."

"Over and out," Caylin said, pushing the off button on the speakerphone. She turned to Theresa and Jo.

Well. So much for getting to bed early. They were going to be up half the night just cleaning up their mistakes, not to mention preparing for the start of their mission.

"Ladies, assume your positions," Jo said. "I think we're in for a long haul."

"The word *oops* seems insufficient at this particular juncture," Caylin remarked. "We screwed up big time."

"We'll have to make it up to The Tower by performing our most heroic deeds yet," Theresa said. It was way too early in her career as a girl spy to get a big black *X* on her permanent record.

"I know this sounds weird, but does anyone else hope that Rosebud is alive?" Caylin asked quietly.

"Yeah," Jo answered. "I mean, sure, the guy tried to kill you and probably would have blown my head off given half a chance . . . but hey, I believe in karma."

"I don't want to kill anyone," Theresa stated simply. "Murder isn't in our job description."

Theresa sighed as she pulled off the tarp closest to her. At this rate the Seattle mission was going to be anything but a snap. As far as she could tell, the Spy Girls were looking at a snap, crackle, pop . . . and fizzle.

"Obliterating any sign that any Spy Girl was a passenger in the gray limousine is a fait accompli," Jo announced upon her return to 902 Stratford Road ninety minutes later. "They haven't invented the piece of high-tech equipment yet that could work its way through the amount of Formula 409 I used on that bad boy of a steering wheel."

Caylin rolled her eyes. "If you're done reveling in your cleaning prowess, Theresa and I have something to show you."

Jo tipped up the brim of her leather poor boy cap. "By all means, O Great Ones."

Caylin tugged at the electric cord she was holding and pushed the plug into the closest outlet. Instantly a bright green neon sign reading

Seattle Sounds lit up the small store. "Ta da!"

Jo whistled softly. Theresa and Caylin had totally transformed the fifteen-hundred-square-foot space during the past hour and a half. "Cool. A record store."

"Correction," Theresa said. "A CD store. And an ultrahip one at that. I don't think you're allowed to buy stuff from here unless you have at least two tattoos and an eyebrow pierce."

Jo glanced around the shop. There was more than a small chance that litters of hot guys would prowl these aisles in the A.M. The place had serious possibilities. "So where do we sleep? In between the Crash Test Dummies and Jim Croce?"

"Uh . . . I think we better call Uncle Sam for an answer to that question," Caylin said. "There's no way I'm going to do the sleeping bag thing tonight."

"It's my turn to reach out and touch someone," Theresa said, stepping toward the speakerphone. "You two have had enough excitement for one grunge night."

Theresa quickly punched in the magic phone number and took a deep breath as she waited for Uncle Sam to answer. "Greetings," she said when she heard the line pick up. "We're ready for our instructions."

"Is it as if that gray limousine never existed at all, Jo?" the boss asked gruffly.

"You've got my word," Jo answered.

"Good." He cleared his throat. "Caylin, there are

three electronic passkeys hidden in a Soundgarden CD case. Find them."

Caylin rifled through a row of CDs, picked out one sans cellophane, and pulled out three small, flat keys. She held them up.

"We've got the keys," Theresa informed the boss.

"Enter the door marked Warehouse," Uncle Sam said tersely. There was a click on the other end of the line and then nothing but a dial tone.

"Cloak-and-daggers continue," Jo commented as the girls dutifully filed toward the twelve-foot-tall steel door at the back of Seattle Sounds. She slid her electronic key into a small slit under the door's heavy metal knob. Instantly the door opened.

Caylin's eyebrows shot up. "Whoa. What looked like your basic CD store . . ."

". . . is actually a front for a high-tech spy operation," Jo finished.

"What a surprise," Theresa added.

Jo stepped inside the center of operations and looked around. The place would have made even 007 weep. There were several fax machines, a dozen phones, and a bunch of weird screens and knobs on the walls. The room was a veritable electronic den. Jo stopped when she realized that a large part of the room's east wall was covered with a screen. And on that screen was a familiar shape—Uncle Sam's shadowy silhouette.

"Welcome, girls," Uncle Sam said. "Have a seat."

As always, his husky voice sent a shiver up Jo's spine. Would she ever see his face?

Jo turned off her hormones and plopped down on the long black leather couch in front of the screen. Theresa and Caylin sat down on either side of her.

"Spy Girls, this is your mission," Uncle Sam began. "You must retrieve and remove a volatile computer code from the mainframe at FutureWorks."

"FutureWorks?" Caylin asked. "It sounds like some kind of company that produces computer games or something."

"Hardly," Uncle Sam answered dryly. "FutureWorks is a Fortune 500 corporation that deals with Internet security."

"Web watchdogs," Theresa explained, looking from Jo to Caylin.

"They're *supposed* to be watchdogs," Uncle Sam concurred. "But in the last two weeks thousands of Internet users have had their credit card numbers stolen—all of whom had made purchases over the Internet using sites patrolled by none other than FutureWorks."

"The plot thickens," Caylin voiced. "But why is this a job for us? I mean, any local outfit could set up some kind of sting to catch whoever is responsible for the thefts."

"Yeah, credit card fraud doesn't seem like a big deal compared to our other missions," Jo observed. She wanted to use her skills and training to save lives, thwart world domination plots, and do her part to clean up the environment. A few stolen credit card numbers didn't exactly spell "global jeopardy."

"Trust me, retrieving this code is a matter of international concern," Uncle Sam said darkly. "Each time the thief—or thieves—steals and encodes another number, the code grows stronger. In a matter of just days every major bank in the world could be rendered powerless . . . and penniless."

Theresa whistled. "The global economy would be shot to you-know-where."

"Governments would collapse and chaos would reign," Uncle Sam corrected her.

"Consider our skepticism retracted," Caylin remarked. "This is the big time."

"So you're ready to hear how I want you to proceed?" Uncle Sam asked, his voice mildly patronizing.

Jo leaned forward. "Tell us everything," she said. The rest of this mission was going to go off without another hitch if she had anything to do with it. One hijacked limousine and a possibly dead bad guy were all the impetus she needed to put her heart and soul into this mission from here on out. "We're ready to work."

Half an hour later Theresa's eyes were drooping shut as the girls signed off. But she couldn't think about bedtime yet. It was imperative that the girls go over Uncle Sam's instructions at least one more time before they went to sleep. No one wanted to risk making another mistake.

Theresa stifled a yawn as she headed up the narrow

spiral staircase that led to their living quarters. "My alias is Tessa Somerset, and I'm a new HTML operator for FutureWorks," she reminded herself aloud. "Tessa Somerset."

Jo followed up close behind, her feet clanging on the metal stairs. "And I'm Julia Martín, espresso maker extraordinaire."

"And I, dear friends, will be known as Courtney Hall, proprietress of Seattle Sounds, for the duration of our stay in the Northwest," Caylin called from the floor.

Theresa had to admit to herself that she felt just a teeny, tiny bit envious of Jo and Caylin. While she toiled away in some corporate cubicle, her friends would be chatting it up with local hipsters. Of course, the assignments made sense.

Mega Mocha, the cafe where Jo would be pouring coffee for foxy guys, was just a couple of blocks away from FutureWorks. There was no doubt that Jo—an expert in, uh, human relations—would be able to eke out pertinent information from FutureWorks employees who stopped by for a caffeine boost. And Caylin would do a great job of keeping the HQ vigil at Seattle Sounds.

"This mission would be a complete bust without you," Jo said, breaking into Theresa's thoughts.

Theresa nodded. Jo was right; Theresa—aka Tessa—was the only Spy Girl with the skills to retrieve the all-important code. Socializing could wait. Theresa had to save the world from financial catastrophe. She brushed away a mental image of the globe collapsing in on itself as she reached the top of the stairs. She opened a plain wooden door.

"Hey, nice crib," Jo said over her shoulder. "If we didn't have to do our spy thang, we could throw a great bash in here."

"Do you think there's a Jacuzzi in the bathtub?" Theresa wondered, walking into the apartment. She was still dreaming of hot water and a fresh bar of soap.

Caylin followed Jo and Theresa into the large living room. "I just hope The Tower provided us with new wardrobes. I'm fresh out of designer duds, as you know."

"Let's investigate," Jo suggested. "Then we'll reconvene for the breakdown."

"Good plan," Theresa agreed.

By midnight the girls had deposited their belongings into the three bedrooms, brushed their teeth, and ground some decaf vanilla hazelnut beans for a pot of genuine Seattle coffee.

Caylin lounged on a short red velvet couch and sipped at an oversize mug of hot coffee. Jo perched on a white leather chair, and Theresa took a seat on the floor. Each girl wore her best let's-get-down-to-business expression.

"So we've all got to be on the lookout for Rosebud," Jo began. "Who knows—maybe the dude is still kickin'." Uncle Sam had told them that Caylin's driver fit the description of Simon Gilbert, the twenty-year-old tech whiz who The Tower suspected might have created the code.

"And we've got to remember that Rosebud was after Theresa in a major way," Caylin said. "He called me 'compu-queen'—obviously he had our identities confused."

Theresa nodded. "Rosebud must have managed to hack into some of The Tower's computer files. He probably knew they were sending me to mess with his ultradevious plans."

"Totally," Caylin agreed. "Ugh—I can't believe that Rosebud guy could have created the code. I mean, how can a dude that scuzzy looking be a genius?"

"*Evil* genius," Theresa stressed. "It takes all kinds."

"Yeah, and this Simon Gilbert dude could spell *b-a-d* bad news," Jo said. "He has a hard-core agenda."

Theresa tried to ignore the shiver that traveled down her spine. Simon Gilbert, Rosebud, *whoever* he was had wanted her dead. And if the guy was brilliant enough to create the code, then he was brilliant enough to have made plans to keep her from completing her mission—even if death intervened in the meantime. Sheesh.

Thank goodness The Tower had already installed an agent at FutureWorks. Agent Vince Trudeau—alias Victor Saunders—had been "working" at the corporation for several months. He had been assigned as an ultimate guard, his job to watch the watchdog. Apparently "Victor" had reported to Uncle Sam that he suspected a breach in security several days ago.

According to Uncle Sam, Victor was almost sure that high-level FutureWorks executives were in on the scam to build a code that would give them access to banks all across the world. He was working hard to uncover the corporate plot, but Victor needed a techie to help with the actual code retrieval. Enter Theresa. Victor would so-called hire her tomorrow morning. And then the fun would begin.

"Basically, Jo and I are in Seattle to cover your back," Caylin said to Theresa. "And to make sure you get out of this thing alive."

"Speaking of alive, let's turn on the news and see if a body was fished out of the Pacific tonight," Jo said with a shudder.

Theresa grabbed the remote control off the top of the art deco coffee table and switched on the TV set. She flipped through three stations, each of which was showing the eleven o'clock news. As far as she could tell, the biggest news event of the day revolved around the new coffee shop that was having its grand opening at a fishermen's wharf in the morning.

"So far, so not so bad," Theresa said. "Nothing on Rosebud or a runaway limousine."

"Let's hope it stays that way," Caylin added.

Theresa turned off the television set. Caylin and Jo could hope all they wanted, but Theresa's gut told her that this mission was going to be their trickiest yet.

"Tessa Somerset, Tessa Somerset," Theresa murmured under her breath as she stood in front of 160 Fleet Street. FutureWorks dominated the entire block, as if the company were an ancient fortress from which soldiers could watch for enemies. Here, Theresa knew, *she* was the enemy.

Mentally sliding into calm, cool, professional Tessa mode, Theresa smoothed her tailored black skirt and tugged at the sleeves of the red Prada jacket she'd found, Tower-supplied and ready to wear, in her closet back at HQ.

Three, two, one.

She walked into the building and headed for the bank of elevators that went to floors twenty-one through thirty. Tessa Somerset, Tessa Somerset. She silently repeated the alias as if it were a mantra as the elevator ascended.

The door opened soundlessly at the thirtieth floor. Theresa stepped out and found herself face to chest with a tall, elegantly dressed man in his late thirties. She knew immediately she was looking at Vince Trudeau, aka Victor Saunders. He had black hair with streaks of gray and a thin, dark mustache.

"Mr. Saunders, I presume," Theresa greeted him, holding out her hand.

"Wonderful to meet you, Tessa," he answered, giving her a firm handshake. "Welcome to FutureWorks."

And it was done. Theresa was an official employee of an official boss. No one else would know that both she and Victor were actually government spies—at least, not until after the mission was completed and all traces of Victor Saunders and Tessa Somerset were permanently erased by The Tower.

As Victor led Theresa to her cubicle he chatted about innocuous subjects: Seattle's relentless fog, the SuperSonics, the coffee fever that had gripped the city since Starbucks opened years ago. "We'll have lunch today to discuss other matters, yes?" Victor suggested eventually.

Theresa nodded. "Of course."

Satisfied, Victor stopped in front of a large cubicle. "Here is your work space, Ms. Somerset. Again, welcome aboard."

"Thank you, Mr. Saunders," Theresa said to her new boss's already retreating back.

"Vic isn't big on socializing," a deep voice informed Theresa. "He's pretty much a nose-to-the-grindstone type."

She turned away from her desk and gave the speaker a once-over. Cute, definitely cute. The guy—sandy brown hair, hazel eyes, and what looked like an athletic build—was sitting at an adjoining desk in her cubicle. His smile was warm and friendly. A welcome surprise.

"I'm Tessa Somerset," she said, shaking the guy's proffered hand.

He grinned. "Brad Fine, resident computer geek."

"Nice to meet you, Brad," she said. Very nice, she thought. Finally Theresa was getting some hot guy action on the job. It was about time.

She slid into her ergonomically correct office chair and booted up the state-of-the-art computer. There was already a pile of work in her in box. Hmmm. It looked like her *real* work was going to have to wait a couple of hours.

Thank goodness Theresa could code HTML in her sleep. The job itself was going to be a bit tedious, but hardly a challenge. As long as she didn't go into a coma from boredom, she would have no problem finding time to crack the code. For several minutes Theresa worked in silence. She stopped typing when an insta-message flashed on the screen of her monitor:

> *How about an early coffee break? I promise to keep the geek factor at no more than a level five.*
>
> *Brad*

Theresa laughed and turned around. "Sounds great—but from one techie to another, you don't have to worry about being a geek around me."

"You mean I can talk about megabytes and RAM capacity?" he asked, his hazel eyes warm and intense.

"As long as you don't mind my obsession with nodes and VirusScan," she responded.

Brad stood up. "Let's blow this Popsicle stand."

Theresa followed without hesitation. After all, getting to know her colleagues was part of the mission. Who knew what kind of vital information was floating around in Brad's oh-so-fine-looking head? Besides, she actually wanted to have some fun. And a little romance wouldn't be a crime.

By eleven o'clock Monday morning Jo had reassessed the difficulty of her job as an international spy. As far as she could make out, working at a popular coffee shop under a boss who had armpit stains and a permanent caffeine high was much more stressful than chasing down assassins.

Mega Mocha was everything a hip cafe was supposed to be. Music blasted from speakers. Seventies memorabilia lined the walls. Young people filled the retro sofas and chairs. In a word, the place was *happening.*

"Am I supposed to twist this nozzle or flip that switch to get the foam to come out right?" Jo asked Doris Fain, a redheaded coworker who seemed to empathize with Jo's inability to make a decent latte.

Doris laughed. "Both." She watched Jo struggle with the nozzle. "Are you sure you've done this before?"

"Sure, I'm sure," Jo said breezily. "But you know how it is . . . no two cappuccino makers are alike!"

Jo turned away from the stainless steel machine and eyed the three guys who had just walked in the door of Mega Mocha. Yum! Maybe hustling coffee had merits Jo hadn't yet considered. She struck her flirt pose—shoulders back, chin up, chest out—and sauntered toward table four.

"Now *this* I know how to do," Jo told Doris over her shoulder.

"Hey, gorgeous," the cutest of the three guys greeted her.

Jo flashed one of her best smiles. *Caray!* This mission would be a total blast—if only she weren't so freaked out about what had happened yesterday. It was hard to enjoy fun and games when she knew there was a distinct possibility that she had helped kill a man.

"I don't know if we have the new Train Slashing Monkeys CD," Caylin said to the girl staring insolently at her from across the counter.

The girl snapped her gum. "You suck."

The customer is always right, Caylin reminded herself as she gave the girl a tight-lipped smile. "I'm sorry . . . I'm kind of new at this."

"What about the Mata Hari Misses?" a guy with a pierced nose inquired. "Do you have the sound track they did for *Evil Man*?"

Caylin shrugged. "Uh, check the new releases section." Man, this job was a minefield. Apparently the entire world of pop culture had passed her by while she had been in training at The Tower.

"Can you order a Def Jack Poppa CD for me?" yet another guy asked. "You're all out."

Across the room a display of CDs crashed to the floor. "Uh, sorry." A skinny guy backed away from the pile of CDs and slunk toward the exit.

Caylin put her hands over her ears and squeezed her eyes shut. The names of a thousand bands she had never heard of before echoed through her brain. This was a nightmare. She'd only been able to slip back to the warehouse once to check for faxes or messages from The Tower, and taking a lunch break seemed pretty much out of the question. Worst of all, Caylin really, *really* had to go to the bathroom.

Aaarrrggghhh!

Theresa chewed on a piece of romaine lettuce from her Chinese chicken salad and listened to Victor intently. He had been speaking almost nonstop for the last fifteen minutes, filling in Theresa on details about FutureWorks that could prove extremely valuable over the next couple of days.

"So tell me more about the Monkey Room," Theresa said before biting into a piece of tender chicken. Mmm. The out-of-the-way, perfect-for-clandestine-meetings restaurant that the V-man had chosen served awesome food. So far today she'd had a good time with a cute guy and been treated to a delicious lunch. Maybe things were looking up.

Victor leaned back and tapped his fingers together. "Ah, yes, the brain center of FutureWorks—known by the peons as the Monkey Room—is the core of company operations."

Theresa nodded. Brad had told her as much during their forty-five-minute midmorning coffee break. She had guessed from Brad's reverent tone during their discussion that the Monkey Room was the key to the mission.

"So how do I get in there?" Theresa asked.

Victor smiled. "I thought you'd never ask." He leaned forward, glancing over his shoulder to make sure that no one was listening. "Unfortunately it's a delicate situation."

Naturally. Nothing was ever *not* delicate when a mission was hanging in the balance. "Tell me everything."

"Security is tight—very tight. Even I don't have clearance to get into the brain center." Victor pushed away his half-eaten Caesar salad and sighed. "And the place is wired like George Orwell's *1984*. There are cameras everywhere."

Great. Wonderful. Terrific. "I'll find a way inside," Theresa promised him. "I know I can."

Victor smiled. "I'm glad you've got such a good attitude, Ms. Somerset." He paused. "I'm handling the administrative side of this, er, problem—you don't have to concern yourself with any of the higher-ups. But you're the only person who can retrieve the code."

"And I will." Theresa wished she felt half as confident as she sounded.

"Just remember to get the code as quickly as possible," Victor said, lowering his voice almost to a whisper. "And then get *out.*" He paused, his face growing grave. "I don't think I need to tell you that you're our only hope."

Theresa shook her head. The weight of the global economy was on her shoulders. From now until the time this mission was over, she had to focus on one thing and one thing only. The code.

Jo had learned more about coffee shops in the last several hours than she had in her entire lifetime. Among other tidbits of information, she had discovered what was commonly known as the midafternoon lull. Ah, yes. That amazing time of day when, apparently, almost no one in the greater Seattle area desired a caffeine jolt. The result of the onset of said lull was that Jo got to sit down for the first time in five hours. A hard, vinyl-covered bar stool had never felt so good.

"Alll III wanna dooo is haave some funnn . . . ," Jo sang along off-key with the CD player as she mindlessly watched the soap opera on the television set over the bar. As far as she could tell, some very attractive guy was mad because some beautiful girl had been kissing another very attractive guy on a set that was supposed to look like a greenhouse but, in fact, looked more like an overgrown Chia garden.

Suddenly the screen went blank. The image of Very Attractive Guy One's angry face was replaced by a fancy logo reading Special Bulletin.

Jo automatically sat up straighter and concentrated on the plastic-looking anchorman who had just appeared on the air. Could be about anything, Jo reminded herself. Maybe there had been a bank robbery or some kind of natural disaster—a typhoon or an earthquake in southern California. Anything was possible. Without sound there was no point in jumping to alarming conclusions.

Again the picture on the television screen changed. The anchorman's face had been replaced with images—uh-oh—of a white limousine being dragged out of the ocean.

Yikes!

Jo's heart pounded as the footage cut to an interview with none other than Travis O'Rourke, her adorable limo driver. Ouch. As cute as Travis's face was, Jo wasn't thrilled to be seeing it on the small screen.

No, the situation was downright awful, Jo realized a moment later. There, for everyone to see, was a police sketch of Jo wearing a headdress—a sketch artist's approximation of her black scarf—and a large pair of sunglasses. Her identity wasn't clear, but the disguise wasn't exactly stellar, either.

A Spy Girl conference was in order. Jo was a wanted woman. And she had no idea how long it would take the police to find her and blow The Tower's mission to smithereens.

Holy moly, Julia!" Doris exclaimed, breaking into Jo's frantic thoughts. "That chick looks just like you!"

"Uh . . ." Jo peered at the sketch even more closely. Oh, man. Doris was right. Any idiot could make a connection between the girl in the sketch and Jo. Words, horrible words, flashed on the screen at the bottom of the sketch.

Doris laughed. "According to the police, you're wanted for grand theft auto and first-degree murder." She patted Jo on the back. "Don't worry, hon. If you get life in prison, I'll bring you a fresh bag of hazelnut beans every week."

Prison. Metal bars. Big, mean women who liked to beat up eighteen-year-old girls. Ugly orange uniforms.

Jo dropped the mug she was holding. It fell to the floor and shattered, splattering coffee across the red-and-white-tile floor.

"Whoa!" Jo exclaimed with a nervous giggle. "Guess I've slammed too much caffeine today . . . my hands are shaking."

Doris nonchalantly glanced at her watch. "Your shift is over, anyway. Why don't you go home and have a cup of decaf?"

Jo laughed again. "Uh, great idea. Decaf. Ha, ha."

In under twenty seconds Jo pulled off her apron, grabbed her backpack from behind the counter, and fled Mega Mocha. She couldn't get back to the safety of HQ fast enough.

Caylin knew that her jaw was practically dragging on the in-need-of-a-sweep-and-mop floor of Seattle Sounds as she stared at one of the televisions that were mounted to the store's ceiling. The news bulletin had, in a phrase, rocked her world.

She was torn between scrambling around to find the remote control so that she could un-mute the sound and standing still so that she wouldn't miss any of the images on-screen. Temporary paralysis dictated the latter. Caylin was absolutely nailed to her spot behind the cash register.

"Who the—?" Yet another picture had flashed across the screen. Caylin had recognized Jo's limo driver, the vehicle, and even the police sketch of Jo. But she had *never* laid eyes on the guy whose picture was currently plastered on the television set. Who was he?

"Did you say something?" The only customer in the shop, a twenty-something guy wearing a University of Washington sweatshirt, glanced from Caylin to the TV to Caylin.

"Uh, no . . . I mean, yeah." She tore her eyes

away from the television set. "I mean, man, there are a lot of wackos out there these days."

"You said it." The guy slapped a CD titled *Rain in July,* by a group called Fungus, onto the counter. "I'll put this on my Visa."

As Caylin rang up the sale—she had finally mastered the cash register sometime between three and four o'clock—thoughts raced through her mind.

There were too many questions. Way too many. Jeez, they didn't even know for certain that Rosebud was actually Simon Gilbert. He could have been anyone. And exactly how did he know to target Theresa? A simple "breach in security" didn't seem to be an adequate explanation.

Caylin tried to ignore the cold knot of dread that had formed in the pit of her stomach. But her gut instincts were usually accurate. And right now her gut was shouting, as if over a loudspeaker, that the disaster surrounding the Spy Girls was even bigger and freakier than anything they had imagined.

"See ya," College Guy said, taking the small plastic bag Caylin held out to him. "Watch out for the psychos."

"If you only knew . . . ," Caylin murmured. She followed the customer to the door, then double-locked it behind him. She didn't care that Seattle Sounds didn't officially close for another two hours. She had to retreat to the warehouse and contact The Tower. Like, yesterday.

* * *

"You can't beat a game of computer Risk," Brad said late Monday afternoon.

Theresa used her mouse to move the rest of her "men" into China. She and Brad had been playing Risk—the object of which was, fittingly enough, world domination—for almost two hours now. He was a formidable opponent and a great conversationalist. As much as Theresa loved Caylin and Jo, she missed being able to discuss the ins and outs of computers with the techie friends she'd had back in Arizona.

"I don't know . . . gaining access to a state-of-the-art mainframe might qualify as more fun," Theresa said. She was justifying her totally non-mission-oriented time with Brad by subtly pumping him for info about the inner workings of FutureWorks.

In the pocket of her jacket Theresa felt her pager vibrate. Probably Caylin and Jo asking her to pick up Chinese food on the way back to HQ, she surmised. Or calling to tell her something incredibly important that could have worldwide implications. Oh, well. She would assume the page was about dinner and continue her fishing expedition uninterrupted.

Brad moved his soldiers into Italy, then leaned back in his chair. "How about going out to dinner with me tonight?" he asked. "There's a great sushi place down at the fishermen's market."

"I'd love to . . . but I can't tonight," Theresa answered. A true enough statement.

"How about tomorrow night?" he pressed. "I can promise you the best yellowtail you've ever had."

"No . . . I don't think so." She wanted to say yes. Theresa really, really wanted to go on a nice, normal date with a nice, normal guy. But she couldn't—not in the middle of a mission.

"What if I told you that I could show you a mainframe that would blow your computer-lovin' mind?" Brad asked. "Please?"

Bingo. Brad knew something significant about the Monkey Room—she had guessed as much this morning when he had told her about it. Theresa could have her date and eat her mission, too. So to speak. "Well . . . okay," she allowed. She *was* human, after all.

"We'll leave right after work," Brad said. "It'll be a night to remember."

And then some. "It's a date," she declared. Smiling to herself, Theresa imagined the many ways the date could end. Maybe she could have some romance *and* save the world, she speculated. A girl could dream . . . later. Right now she had to conquer the rest of Asia.

"Did we page her, or did we page her?" Caylin asked Jo.

Jo shrugged. "We paged her. Twice."

The girls had locked themselves into the warehouse, where they were keeping a TV news vigil. The Seattle police chief had announced earlier that he would hold a press conference at 4:45 P.M., and

Jo and Caylin were waiting for it to begin. They had agreed to hold off on contacting Uncle Sam until they knew as much as possible about what was going on.

"Maybe Theresa doesn't realize how much trouble we're in," Jo suggested. "She's probably been locked in some tiny, over-air-conditioned cubicle all day."

"She should be here," Caylin insisted. There was strength in numbers, and the Spy Girls needed every iota of strength they could muster.

From earlier reports Caylin and Jo had pieced together the police department's theory of last night's events. Detectives believed that Jo, Caylin, and Theresa were part of a girl gang and that the crime had been a quote bizarre female gang heist unquote.

"I thought they quit using the word *heist* around the time that Bonnie and Clyde kicked the bucket," Jo commented.

"Call it whatever you want," Caylin responded. "They still think you're a cold-blooded killer."

Every word of the news report was imprinted upon Caylin's memory:

"Last night members of a female gang wreaked havoc on the city of Seattle. One of the members stole a gray limousine at gunpoint, then, according to reports, proceeded on a mad car chase. This morning a white limousine was found in the Pacific. A man, identified as twenty-three-year-old Seth Armstrong,

was found dead inside the vehicle. Police are looking for suspects as well as for the gray limousine. . . ."

Ugh.

"The man who died was definitely *not* Rosebud," Jo said for the fifth time.

"Nope," Caylin agreed. "I got a good look at Rosebud—*too* good. That guy in the picture they showed wasn't anyone I've ever seen before."

"Which means that the murder victim was probably Theresa's *real* limo driver." Jo chewed on her thumbnail and stared into space. Caylin could practically see her mind working overtime.

"Rosebud killed the driver," Caylin said. "That much seems obvious."

Jo shuddered. "And he would have killed you if he'd had the chance." She sat up straighter. "Hey, the press conference is starting." Jo leaned forward and turned up the volume on the television set.

On the TV screen the stern-looking police chief, Officer Bascovitz, cleared his throat. "At the current time we are trying to locate three females," Officer Bascovitz announced. "Two are suspected of homicide."

"Two?" Caylin squeaked.

The police chief held up two sketches, and the camera zoomed in on them. They were clearly sketches of Jo and Caylin, although both wore their cheesy disguises.

"A third female may have been abducted from the scene of the crime," Officer Bascovitz continued. He held up yet another police sketch. This one was of Theresa, but most of her face was hidden by an enormous pair of mirrored aviator sunglasses. "An eyewitness claims to have seen one of the suspects order the third female into the missing gray limousine."

"Gulp," Jo said. "Could the news get *any* worse?"

"We have recovered a handgun from the scene," the officer informed reporters.

"Yes, things *could* get worse—and they just have." Caylin forced herself to look at the bright side. At least none of the Spy Girls' fingerprints could be on the handgun the cops found. Guns were *not* part of their Tower-approved paraphernalia.

On TV, Officer Bascovitz cleared his throat again. "We have found items belonging to one of the suspects in the white limousine," he said. "From an item of clothing discovered in those belongings, we will attempt to make a positive ID on the suspect. As soon as that ID has been made, we will put out an all-points bulletin."

Caylin froze. An item of clothing . . . oh no. Her lucky cap. Officer Bascovitz had been referring to her yellow Sunset Hill School baseball cap. Caylin was sure of it. She was dead meat. Stupid, stupid, stupid!

"A further search for bodies revealed nothing," the officer finished. "We can only hope that there will be no more deaths at the hands of these evil young women." He paused. "The public should be aware that these girls are considered armed and extremely dangerous. Treat them as such."

Mercifully the press conference ended, and Caylin switched off the TV set. Her lucky baseball cap . . . the one with the logo of her boarding school emblazoned across its front. Bringing the cap along on her Spy Girl missions had been a serious error.

"We might as well chop ourselves into tiny pieces and stuff each other into a garbage disposal," Jo said glumly.

"Rosebud is still out there," Caylin commented. "If he had died in the limo, the police would have found him."

Jo sighed dramatically. "Uncle Sam isn't going to like this latest news flash—not at all."

"I take back wishing that Rosebud didn't kick it in the ocean," Caylin announced.

"I'm with you there," Jo agreed. "He could ruin the whole mission—not to mention our *lives.*"

"We have to call The Tower," Caylin said. "Uncle Sam is the only person who might be able to get us out of this atomic situation."

"We'll get in touch with him soon," Jo agreed. "But first we need to talk to Theresa."

Caylin nodded. "The one thing we know for sure is that Rosebud wants Theresa six feet under. Until this blows over, her life is in grave danger."

She dialed the main number for FutureWorks, praying that Theresa would answer her desk phone. All the while Caylin kept avoiding the only reason why Theresa wouldn't respond to their pages. She wouldn't allow herself to think that Rosebud had already struck.

Theresa really didn't want to answer the ringing phone on her desk. She was flirting for the first time in months, and flexing the old womanly wile muscles felt darn good. Unfortunately she couldn't ignore the possibility that the call pertained to the mission.

She picked up the receiver. "Hello. This is Tessa Somerset."

"What are you *doing?*" Caylin squealed on the other end of the line. "Jo and I are *freaking* out. We thought you were *dead!*"

Theresa held the phone away from her ear for a moment's relief from Caylin's high-pitched screech. "Sorry . . . I've been, uh, busy." She glanced at the Risk board on her computer screen. Okay, maybe "busy" was an exaggeration. But still. There was no point in going postal.

"FYI, Rosebud is alive, Jo and I are wanted for murder, and the cops think we kidnapped you."

"What?" Theresa shrieked. She glanced at Brad, who looked alarmed. "I mean, what?" she whispered into the phone.

"You heard me," Caylin said. "Now get your butt back to HQ so we can figure out how to proceed. Okeydoke?"

Theresa gulped. Oops. She'd never ignore her

pages again. "I'll be there in twenty minutes," she promised.

Her hands shook as she hung up the phone. Brad was staring at her, questions in his warm hazel eyes. "My roommate . . . says my cat is sick," Theresa explained lamely. "I, uh, need to take her to the vet."

Brad glanced at his watch. "We're not off for another half hour. They're pretty strict about the time clock around here."

Theresa locked eyes with Brad. "Well, since Victor and I are actually working together as international spies, I'm pretty sure he'll let me go home early." She winked.

Brad laughed. "Funny girl," he said admiringly.

She knocked lightly on the door of Victor's office, then poked her head inside. He was talking intently into the telephone, his voice low. When Victor saw her, he hung up the telephone immediately. "Yes?" he asked.

"Victor—I've got to go," Theresa said. "We're having something of a meltdown back at HQ."

Victor didn't ask any questions. He merely nodded. "I'm handling things here. Go home and take care of business."

Theresa closed the door thoughtfully. Victor hadn't seemed surprised by her request to leave work early. He hadn't even inquired as to whether or not she had made progress with the code. Was it possible that he already knew about the allegations against Caylin and Jo? If so, why hadn't he told her?

Turning the question over in her mind, Theresa walked back to her cubicle and grabbed her small leather briefcase. "I got the green light," she informed Brad. "I'm outta here."

"Wow!" Brad exclaimed. "Victor must really like you. He's never let *me* go home early."

"What can I say? He's a cat lover." And with that cryptic exit line, she split.

As the sun set over Seattle, Jo, Caylin, and Theresa locked themselves in the warehouse, away from anything that might distract them from their immediate goal: getting their butts out of some seriously hot water.

Jo stared at Uncle Sam's shadowy figure on the huge screen and wished that he would offer the girls a magic exit out of this giant pothole in their mission. No such luck. "At least you girls know that you're not responsible for anyone's death," Uncle Sam was saying. "Simon Gilbert is still alive."

"But the cops think we're *guilty,*" Jo exclaimed. "We're being framed!"

"Calm down, Jo," Uncle Sam ordered. "The Tower will clear up this misunderstanding once the mission is completed."

"You want us to go ahead with the mission?" Caylin squeaked. "Don't you think that's a little unwise under the present circumstances?"

"So far, the police don't know who any of you are," Uncle Sam said. "As of now, I want you to proceed with the mission as planned."

Theresa looked up from the top secret computer decoding manual she had received from operatives at The Tower. "I met a guy at work who's going to show me around FutureWorks tomorrow," she informed Uncle Sam. "I think Brad knows how to get into the Monkey Room."

"The Monkey Room?" Uncle Sam asked skeptically. "Sounds like a come-on line to me."

"He's for real!" Theresa insisted. "Victor verified that FutureWorks plebs have nicknamed the main brain center the Monkey Room."

"How do you know this Brad can be trusted?" Uncle Sam asked.

Jo noticed a light pink blush spreading across Theresa's face. Hmmm. Interesting. Was it possible that in the midst of this turmoil Theresa was falling for a fellow computer nerd?

"I know how to judge character," Theresa insisted. "Brad's an upstanding guy—and he knows almost as much as I do about hard drives."

"Well, just make sure you don't get caught up in some kind of techie prank," Uncle Sam said.

Caylin snorted. "Yeah, the last thing we need is the Bradster trying to impress you by posting some fake letter from the president on some White House web page or something."

Theresa glared at Caylin. "We can quit discussing Brad now," she snapped. "I have one concern and one concern only. I'm going to get the code and get out."

"I don't think I need to emphasize that time is

of the essence, Theresa." Uncle Sam's voice was stern—more stern than Jo had ever heard it.

"I *know*," Theresa said. "Sheesh, I'm doing everything I can."

"Stay safe, girls. Over and out." Typical. Uncle Sam wasn't big on warm and fuzzy good-byes. A moment after the succinct *sayonara* the screen went blank.

"At least the boss isn't totally wigging," Caylin commented. "I guess we should find comfort in his calm."

"Yeah, well, *he's* not the one being framed for first-degree, wham bam, see ya, wouldn't want to be ya, man." Since this afternoon Jo hadn't been able to get the image of herself in an ill-fitting jumpsuit and clunky leg irons out of her mind.

"He's also not the one with a psycho killer after his Tower tail," Theresa added.

Jo bit her lip, resisting the urge to chew her fingernails down to the quick. They couldn't despair. Not now. One false move could equal a major catastrophe . . . for them and for the world.

"Can we all take a moment and thank the pizza gods?" Caylin asked. "Aside from a chocolate bar and half a rank cup of blueberry yogurt, this is the first thing I've eaten all day." She took another bite of the now piping hot pizza they had found in the stocked freezer, savoring a thick piece of pepperoni.

Jo pushed away her plate. "I have no appetite. It feels like there's a Nerf ball in my stomach."

Theresa looked up from a Tower textbook titled *The Seven Habits of Highly Effective Hackers.* "I think it's time to call in the troops, if you know what I mean."

"Are you suggesting we put our pride where the sun don't shine and call Danielle?" Caylin asked.

Jo nodded. "You got it, babe." She looked from Theresa to Caylin. "All in favor, say, 'SOS.'"

"SOS," Caylin and Theresa responded in stereo. If Jo hadn't suggested calling Danielle, Caylin would have in a heartbeat.

Danielle, otherwise known as Glenda the Good Witch, was the Spy Girls' guardian angel. A veteran Tower agent, Danielle often swooped down to give the girls advice when they were stuck between a rock and a big black abyss. The woman was like a walking, talking international spy guide.

"I'll make the call," Caylin offered. She licked pizza sauce off her fingers and dialed Danielle's number on the nearest speakerphone.

A moment later the knightess in shining armor answered the phone. "Hey, it's the teen dream team!" she greeted them. "Caught any bad guys lately?"

The girls' collective groan was answer enough. "Uh-oh," Danielle said. "From the desolate tone of your youthful voices, I'm speculating that this problem is worse than a run in your panty hose."

"We're toast," Caylin answered. "We're burnt toast with butter and jam and the crusts cut off."

"Tell me everything," Danielle said.

Caylin started the story. Theresa supplied the middle. And Jo finished off with the bummer news that she and Caylin were wanted for murder and Theresa was quite possibly the target of a trigger-happy madman.

"I think it's fairy-dust time," Danielle said when they finished their tale of woe. "You girls need help in a big way."

"Exactly," Caylin said. "Got any suggestions?"

"The frame-up will get resolved in the long run," Danielle said. "As Sam told you, The Tower will make sure that you all are cleared."

"But in the short run we've got a bunch of local yokels with sheriff's badges wanting our butts in the electric chair," Jo pointed out.

"Okay, here's the plan," Danielle said in the crisp, firm voice that meant she was about to issue orders that she didn't want questioned. "Jo and Caylin, you two need makeovers." She paused. "I want totally new hair for Caylin and Jo. I want you girls to go heavy on the funky makeup and scanty in the clothes department."

"Uh . . . okay," Caylin responded. She wasn't thrilled at the idea of dyeing her hair, but it was a heck of a lot better prospect than sticking her thumbs in an ink pad at the police station.

"What about me?" Theresa asked. "Everyone at FutureWorks is going to think I'm nuts if I show up for my second day of work looking like an escapee from Hole."

"You're right, Theresa," Danielle agreed. "The police's ID of you is the least secure, and as far as they're concerned you've been hidden away somewhere. They won't be looking for you. So just continue at FutureWorks as if you don't have a care in the world."

"Check," Theresa said. "Not a care in the world . . . yeah, *right.*"

"Good luck, Spy Queens," Danielle said. "I have every confidence that you all will come out of this with flying colors—and not just in your hair."

"I hope you're right," Caylin said. "But right now this feels like it could very well be our last mission."

"Don't let negative energy keep you girls down," Danielle said in her best pep-talk voice. "Go get 'em, and remember that a good attitude is half the battle."

Caylin clicked off the phone. "Looks like we need an all-night drugstore," she said. "Two boxes of hair dye coming up."

Theresa stood. "I'll go—the cops are combing the streets for you guys."

"The cops are combing the streets, and we'll be combing our hair." Jo laughed weakly. "It makes a certain amount of crazy sense."

"Let's hope a couple of new hairdos will be enough," Caylin suggested. "I'm not up for major plastic surgery." She felt the three pieces of pizza she had eaten congealing in her stomach. The Spy Girls were all safe for now. But as of tomorrow, they would be back out on the streets . . . where anything could happen. A box of hair dye wasn't going to change that fact.

Theresa prowled through the aisles of an all-night drugstore, tossing items into her blue plastic basket. If the circumstances weren't so dire, this shopping spree would have been kind of fun. Purchasing large amounts of cheap makeup was liberating.

She surveyed the contents of the basket: all colors of eye shadow, mascara, and lipstick; temporary tattoos; black hair dye; blond hair dye; red hair dye; two streak kits. What else did she need?

Theresa kept her eyes glued to the stocked aisles as she walked. Who knew there were so many beauty products on the market? Bikini wax treatments, mustache bleach, blackhead strips, cucumber masks, fingernail strengtheners, eyelash curlers. There was no end to the number of items a girl could buy to make herself more attractive to the opposite sex. Theresa's own beauty regime consisted of soap and water and moisturizer, period.

"Ummph." Theresa bumped into a large, solid figure next to her. Whoops. She had been so lost in her musings that she had mistakenly wandered into the men's hygiene section.

"Tessa?" Oh, man. Brad! Talk about dumb luck—or lack thereof.

"Brad! Hi!" Theresa smiled innocently, she

hoped, and tried to mentally quell the quickening of her heartbeat. He looked even cuter in Levi's and an old T-shirt than he had in khakis and a button-down.

"How's the cat?" he asked.

The cat? Theresa racked her brain. "Oh, the *cat.*" She giggled nervously. "Fluffy is fine. She just, uh, swallowed a hair ball . . . no problem."

He grinned. "So we're still on for tomorrow night? You're not going to have to keep a vigil by Fluffy's sickbed or anything?"

Theresa shook her head. "Absolutely not. She's back to her old self—she, uh, even killed a mouse tonight."

"So what are you doing here?" Brad asked.

"Who, me?" Theresa asked. "I was, um, out of toothpaste. And shampoo. And a couple of other things." She took off in the direction of the pet food aisle. "Actually, I needed to get a new brand of cat food for Fluffy—one the vet suggested."

Brad glanced into her overflowing basket. "Are you also planning on opening a beauty salon?" he asked as they headed down aisle six. "I don't think I've ever seen so much makeup and stuff in one place."

She stared guiltily into her basket. "Um, I'm throwing a girlie party this weekend—you know, one of those chick-bonding nights when we get together and do each other's hair and makeup." She'd never done anything like that in her life, but the explanation seemed to satisfy Brad.

They reached the pet food aisle. Theresa tossed several cans of Feline Feast into her basket. Now *there* was something she'd never use.

"So, are you ready to pay?" Brad asked. "We can chat about gigabytes while we wait in line."

Think fast, Tessa, Theresa told herself. There was no way she could let Brad watch her pay for her loot. She had zero cash, which meant she had to use her Tower credit card. The leftover one from London that had the collective Tower alias Camilla Stevens stamped across the front.

"Uh, I've still got to pick up a few more things," she said.

"No prob. I'll keep you company." Brad put his hand on her back, as if to guide her toward her destination.

Theresa started to walk aimlessly. She *had* to get rid of him, much as she would have liked to stay and flirt. Brainstorm! She changed directions and headed toward the dreaded feminine hygiene aisle. Theresa stopped in front of a row of tampons and pads and started to do some price comparing. "Hey, Brad? Which of these do you think—"

Right on cue, Brad's face matched the blue lipstick Theresa had stashed away in her basket. "I've, uh, got to get home," he said, averting his eyes from a box of Always with wings. "I'll see you at work tomorrow morning."

Theresa smiled. Thank goodness testosterone precluded the other half from being able to deal with a biological process that was as natural as breathing. Sometimes a girl needed to be left alone. Forget the pizza gods. Right now Theresa was praising the fertility goddesses. She was home free!

"I thought we were going to dye my hair *black*," Caylin moaned as she stared at her candy apple red hair in the bathroom mirror.

"You would have looked like Elvira if your hair were black," Jo pointed out. "Red suits you."

Caylin groaned. "I'd rather look like Elvira than Bozo The Clown."

Jo looked thoughtfully at her own makeover. A bottle-opening mishap had sent the superlightening blond color down the shower drain. Since the red hair dye had gone to Caylin, Jo had been forced to make do with both streak kits and the bottle of blue-black.

"I look like a skunk," Jo announced. "But I like it."

"Everyone in Seattle has weird hair," Theresa commented. "Don't worry about it."

"You wouldn't be saying that if *your* hair looked like something out of *The Simpsons*," Caylin said. "Brad might not like it if your luxurious brunette hair suddenly resembled a cheap, acrylic wig."

"Who knows?" Jo teased. "Maybe he's the kinky type."

Theresa sighed. "Can we shut up about Brad and do a final security check?" she asked. "Unlike you two, I have *real* work to do in the morning."

Caylin and Jo nodded in unison. The idea of going to bed was too tantalizing a prospect to pass up. "I'll do a twice-over on the windows," Caylin offered.

"And I'll check the doors," Jo said. "Again."

"Put me down for the alarm system," Theresa offered. "Thank goodness for motion detectors."

The trio filed out of the marble-tiled bathroom, and each Spy Girl headed for her designated security post. Caylin pulled on each of the apartment's windows, making sure that no intruder could get inside via the fire escape. At the last window she stopped and peered into the dark night. Rosebud was out there . . . somewhere. And until they knew who he was, where he was, and what he wanted, not one of them was safe.

up. "I'll do it tomorrow on the way back," Casey offered.

"And I'll call the agency," Dustin said. Again [illegible]

"[illegible] time for the [illegible]," [illegible] offered. "Thanks, and [illegible] for [illegible]."

[illegible] the [illegible] of the [illegible] and each [illegible] for her [illegible] my [illegible] pulled on each of the [illegible] windows, making sure that no [illegible] could get inside [illegible] the [illegible] as the [illegible] and [illegible] into the dark [illegible] was out there [illegible]. And [illegible] they knew who he was, where he was, and what he wanted, not one of them was safe.

"I said baaayybeee, are you gonna something-something saaave meee," Jo sang tunelessly as she carried a loaded tray to table twelve on Tuesday morning. Mega Mocha was packed, but Jo had more or less gotten the hang of her waitressing-slash-coffee-goddess gig. It was actually kind of a kick.

She stopped in front of the table full of preteens, who were most likely skipping school.

"Nice streaks," a tall blond guy commented from the next table. "You've got a total rock chick thang happening."

Jo batted her heavily mascara-coated eyelashes. "Thanks, blondie. Maybe I'll do *your* hair sometime." She shifted her attention to her customers. "I've got café au lait. I've got café mocha. I've got a double espresso." She set down the drinks in front of the kids.

"Hey, you're improving," remarked one of the girls. She had been in the cafe yesterday, at which point Jo had accidentally served her an iced coffee instead of coffee ice cream.

Jo grinned. "Thanks—and don't forget to tip," she suggested. "Gratuity is next to godliness." Man, it was nice to feel like a normal, teenage waitress. Sure, being a spy had tons of perks, but occasionally the concept of living a mundane, *Regis and Kathie Lee*–watching life was enticing.

"Excuse me, ma'am. May I seat myself?" The overly polite question had been asked by none other than Theresa.

Jo turned around. "Why, yes, miss, sit wherever you like. There's a lovely table by the window." She waved her order pad in Theresa's face. "I'll be with you in a moment."

But Theresa didn't sit down. She was staring intently at something over Jo's shoulder.

"Cute guy at twelve o'clock?" Jo asked.

"Not exactly."

Jo pivoted and followed the direction of Theresa's gaze. Uh-oh. Chapter two. There was another news bulletin on the television set. From the images on the screen it was obvious that the station was offering an update on the so-called girl gang.

"Turn it up!" someone shouted from table nine. "This story rocks!"

"Yeah! We want to hear about the chick killers!" another customer yelled from a plush red velvet sofa.

"Okay, okay!" Doris yelled. "I give!" She switched off the CD that had been blasting through the speakers and turned up the volume on the TV set.

"The blond female gang member has been identified as seventeen-year-old Caylin Pike," the newscaster announced. "Her name was traced through a high school yearbook from her alma mater, the prestigious Sunset Hill School." Instantly a photo of Caylin on her high school graduation day—looking *très* adorable in cap and gown—flashed across the screen.

"The suspect may look harmless," the anchorwoman continued. "But we stress that she and her cohort *are* considered armed and extremely dangerous."

Their cover was blown to bits. That much was clear.

"Is this really happening?" Jo whispered.

"Pike's parents were unavailable for comment," the anchorwoman continued. "But we will be sure to keep the public updated on the unfolding events of this most troubling story."

"This is happening, all right," Theresa said softly. "We'd better warn Caylin."

"I'll call her," Jo offered. "And you and I better steer clear of each other."

"I'll get my java to go," Theresa agreed. "Call me with developments."

As Theresa walked to the counter to order her coffee, Jo sped through the crowded cafe and parked herself next to the pay phone outside the women's bathroom. She pulled one of her tip quarters out of her apron pocket and dropped it into the coin slot. She quickly dialed the number for HQ, which she knew would also ring in Seattle Sounds.

The phone rang six times before Caylin finally picked up. "Hello!" she shouted. In the background Jo could hear a Garbage CD playing at top volume. "Seattle Sounds, Courtney speaking."

"Hi, Courtney. It's Julia." Jo tapped her pen against the side of the phone as she waited for Caylin to turn down the music.

"What's up?" Caylin asked a moment later. "And don't tell me you're in jail, using your one phone call."

From the other side of the cafe Jo could see Doris staring at her. Okay. She had to make this rap session quick and to the point. "Things aren't that bad—yet," Jo said quietly. "But do yourself a favor—don't watch the news today."

She hung up before Caylin could respond. Doris seemed to be genuinely friendly and on the level, but a Spy Girl could never be too careful. The last thirty-six hours had taught her *that* painful lesson.

Caylin dropped the phone into its Day-Glo orange cradle. Jo hadn't said much—she hadn't needed to. Caylin turned the music down even lower and cupped her hands around her mouth.

"I'm sorry, but, uh, Seattle Sounds is closed for the next hour," she announced to the customers, who were pawing aimlessly through the CDs. "We've got an, uh, emergency plumbing problem."

Caylin couldn't see any reason not to close the store for a while. So far, her job had been more about ringing up sales and answering idiotic questions than it had been about gathering and disseminating information.

One girl drifted toward the door, hauling her boyfriend along with her. Two other guys kept flipping through CDs as if Caylin hadn't spoken.

"I said get *out*," she seethed. Running a store took way too much patience. She'd had it with that stupid customer-is-always-right credo. "*Now.*"

The guys looked at each other and shrugged. "Okay, Red, we get the message," one of them said. "Man, this town used to be *friendly*."

As soon as the guys were gone Caylin shoved the Closed sign in the window and locked the door. She walked to the back of the store and slipped into the warehouse, where she could watch the news in private. It didn't take long to surmise why Jo had called with the warning. Every station in the city was airing her high school graduation photo.

Tears sprang to Caylin's eyes when she flipped to a channel that was showing a different picture. In the photograph Caylin was standing between her parents, who were smiling proudly for the camera. She remembered having that photo taken—it had meant a lot to her to get a picture of the whole family together. Even though her parents' divorce had been as amicable as a divorce *could* be, moments of true togetherness were now few and far between.

Caylin grabbed the portable phone and dialed Uncle Sam's direct number. "I have to call my parents," she said as soon as she heard his husky voice. "The cops know who I am, and I'm sure reporters are hounding my mom and dad."

"Absolutely not," Uncle Sam said firmly. "Contacting your family at this juncture would be a critical error. There's every possibility that their phone lines are being tapped."

"So you know what's going on?" Caylin asked. "You know that they traced me to Sunset Hill?"

"We know everything," Uncle Sam said. "And we're doing all we can. I know it's tough, but you've got to proceed as we discussed."

Caylin fought back tears as she hung up the phone. She felt utterly defeated. Reaching over to turn off the TV, she suddenly froze. There were her parents. Both of them. They were standing in front of the home she grew up in, and there were a dozen reporters sticking microphones in their faces.

"Mrs. Pike, where is your daughter?" one reporter shouted. "Has she tried to contact you in any way?"

"Were there signs that your daughter was involved in gang activity?" another reporter demanded.

"Caylin is innocent," Mr. Pike told the reporters. "That's all we have to say."

"Do you know where she is?" the first reporter asked again. "Are you aware that harboring a fugitive makes you an accessory to murder?"

"Our daughter has done nothing wrong," Mrs. Pike said, her voice strained but calm. "We have no further comment."

A tear slid down Caylin's face as she watched her parents join hands and turn to walk back into the house. With every fiber of her being she longed to call and assure them that she was, in fact, innocent. She knew they were going through agony . . . they had to be. She reached for the phone, then dropped her hand.

"I can't call them," Caylin said aloud. "I can't disobey a direct order." She sighed deeply. The little girl inside her wanted nothing more than to crawl onto her mother's lap for comfort. But she wasn't a little girl anymore, and she couldn't pretend that Mommy could make everything all better. Caylin was a Spy Girl, and she had a mission to accomplish.

Taking a deep breath, Caylin prepared herself to go back into the store and reopen for business. There was work to do.

Theresa pushed enter on her keyboard and glanced at her in box. Empty. She had completed her morning's work in record time. Which left Theresa free to go after the code.

Or flirt with Brad. She noticed out of her peripheral vision that he had just pushed his chair away from his desk and swiveled in her direction.

"Hey, Tessa? Sorry I ran out on you so fast last night," Brad said haltingly. He ran a hand through his thick sandy brown hair. "I just, uh, realized I had to get home."

Yeah, right, she thought. The fact that he was standing in front of a panoramic display of tampons and maxi pads had nothing to do with it. "No problem," Theresa assured him.

"So, did you catch the news last night?" he asked. "There's some pretty disturbing stuff going on in this city."

"Um, yeah. I mean, no. I don't watch the news. . . . I, uh, prefer the Discovery Channel." She had no desire to get drawn into a discussion about local current events.

"There's like this wild girl gang on the prowl," Brad said excitedly. "They've killed at least one guy, and they may have kidnapped a girl."

Time to change the subject, Theresa told herself. Brad's inquiring mind needed to be stopped. "Um, what are you doing for lunch?" she asked, ignoring his comments completely. "I was thinking about going to that little bistro around the corner."

Brad's face fell. "I'd love to go with you, but I have an appointment."

"Oh, well," Theresa said breezily. "I'd probably be better off catching up on my employee's manual reading, anyway." Uh-huh, she added silently. She always spent her free time reading about the rules and regulations regarding worker dress code. Not!

In *veritas*, she was psyched to have some Brad-free hacking time. Cute or not, the guy seemed to have a million pairs of eyes watching her every move. Besides, they would have plenty of time to rap on their date.

"By the way, what have you got planned for tonight?" she asked.

Brad's hazel eyes sparkled. "That, my computer geek friend, is a secret."

Theresa raised her eyebrows. "Sounds fascinating."

"It'll be a night to remember, all right," Brad agreed. He reached into the pocket of his tweed sports coat and pulled out a tiny camera. "Say, 'cheese!'"

Before Theresa could respond, he had snapped her photograph with what she recognized to be a digital camera. Terrific. This wasn't the best time for a photo op. "What was that for?" she asked quickly.

Brad slipped the camera back into his pocket. "I'm not at liberty to say . . . but you'll find out soon enough."

Theresa turned back to her monitor.

Hmmm.

Jo appraised her appearance in the small, smoky mirror over the sink in the women's bathroom. This would be her last chance to reapply lipstick before the lunch rush slammed every waitress in Mega Mocha.

Not bad. Not bad at all. The peroxide blond and blue-black streaks in her dark hair lent her a dangerous edge that appealed to her sense of adventure.

With this hairdo who knew what kind of thrills were in store for her? Anything was possible. Plus nobody would suspect a girl with much makeup of being an undercover operative. Jaclyn Smith, she most certainly was *not.*

Jo tucked the tube of Darkly Sensuous lipstick into her apron pocket, checked to make sure her high-tech mascara cam—an essential for any spy worth her weight in espresso beans—was still where she could get at it with one swift grab, and prepared to face the pit bulls. Seattlites desperately in need of a java fix were an angry breed.

She pushed open the door of the bathroom, sauntered back to the counter, and surveyed the crowd. Grunged-out teenagers lounged on sofas and fraying recliners. Young professionals sipped coffee as they thumbed through *The Wall Street Journal.* A few random mothers ordered bagels by the dozen as screaming babies tugged at their hair. Yep. As usual, the place looked alarmingly free of any kind of mission-related activity.

"Get a load of the guy at table five," Doris said, nudging Jo. "He is *h-o-t.* At least from this angle." She poked Jo again. "And he's sitting in *your* section."

Jo nodded absently. Yes, in an ideal world she would have nothing better to do than stand around and analyze the physical merits of every guy who happened to walk into Mega Mocha. But if something relating to the covert didn't happen soon, she was going to think this whole coffee-pouring gig was a bust.

"Then again, I'm not sure I dig that tattoo on the back of his neck," Doris said. "Creep-o-rama."

Jo felt her left eye twitch.

Tattoo.

Neck.

Was it possible in any way, shape, or form that . . . ?

No.

Jo glanced over at table five. Instantly her heart sped up to a rate of approximately a thousand beats a second. The guy sitting at table five had a tattoo on the back of his neck, all right. A tattoo of a rosebud.

Whoa. Hold the phone. Covert action had arrived with a bang.

While she stood with her mouth hanging open, a guy walked into Mega Mocha and plopped into the chair opposite Rosebud's. Jo didn't know who he was, but if the dude was here to meet up with Rosebud, he had to be bad news.

"Show time," Jo whispered. Taking a deep breath, she went for it.

Access denied. Password not recognized. User not known.

"Dang." Theresa kicked the side of her desk with the heel of her black pump in frustration. FutureWorks didn't take many chances with its security system—well, security *was* their business, after all. A total genius must have programmed the mainframe. It was becoming all too obvious that she wasn't going to get inside the computer nerve center without some heavy-duty hacking gear.

There was a military-authorized pass code detector disk in her leather briefcase. Would it be safe to insert the disk into the A drive?

She glanced around, looking for anyone who might be poised to see untoward behavior. There was no one.

She continued to sweep the area with watchful eyes. Huh. A smoke detector was mounted in a ceiling corner. The detector looked standard, but Theresa wasn't going to take any risks. Hadn't Victor told her that there were cameras all over FutureWorks?

She stared at the smoke detector, rubbing one of her eyes as if there were something in it. There was no reason to arouse suspicions by ogling a hidden camera. Yep . . . there it was. A tiny red dot showed between the slats of the detector. Bingo.

Theresa turned back to her computer. She couldn't do any big-time hacking at her desk. She would have to take the show on the road . . . or in this case down the hall. She gathered up her belongings as if she were headed off to lunch. Just call me Sneaky Spice, she thought. FutureWorks was her stage. But she didn't want any spotlight shining on her . . . yet.

"That'll be twenty-six seventy-four," Caylin said to the brown-haired guy who stood on the other side of the cash register. She glanced at his CD choice. *Evita.* "Let me guess . . . it's a present for your girlfriend, right?"

He grinned. "How'd you guess?"

Caylin laughed, feeling something approaching lighthearted for the first time in two days. "Musical sound tracks aren't too popular among the male half of the species."

The guy took his purchase. "Have a great day. I'll be back for that Manhattan Madness CD when it comes in."

Caylin waved good-bye, feeling slightly proud of herself. Sure, she had screwed up her parents' lives, put the entire mission in jeopardy, and was wanted for first-degree murder. But dang if she wasn't turning out to be one heck of a CD store proprietress.

The bell over the front door jangled, and Caylin looked up from the receipts she was organizing. Two men walked inside. Correction. Two *police*men walked inside, decked out in full men-in-blue garb, billy clubs at their sides. Talk about a sorry—no, *scary*—sight to see.

Police. Cops. Fuzz. The keepers of the thin blue line. She was in for it. Caylin was torn between standing up tall and proud as if she had nothing to hide and shrinking into her skin in order to be as inconspicuous as possible. She settled on a posture somewhere in between—head up, shoulders hunched. Not the best look for an international spy. And now the cops were heading straight in her direction.

I plead the fifth. I demand my lawyer, she told them silently. But Caylin didn't have a lawyer. Oh, well. Her heart pounded as the men approached. "Hello, Officers," she greeted them. "What can I do for you?" The best defense was a good offense, or so the saying claimed.

"Hiya, miss." One of the policemen held out his hand. "I'm Officer Denver."

"Hi. Courtney Hall." Caylin shook his outstretched hand and thanked the beauty industry—and Danielle—for red hair in a box. She also gave a silent thanks to Jo for forcing her to put a huge butterfly temporary tattoo on her arm. The clip-on nose ring had been Caylin's own idea. The men didn't seem to recognize her. So far.

The other cop extended his hand. "Officer Barkman, ma'am."

Ma'am? That was a new one.

"What can I help you guys with?" Caylin asked, grateful that previous missions had given her experience in the my-voice-isn't-trembling-even-though-my-knees-are-knocking territory.

"We noticed that Seattle Sounds is a new shop in town," Officer Denver said. "We wanted to come by and welcome you to the neighborhood."

"Well, thanks, that was mighty nice of y'all." Caylin knew that stupidity could go a long way in the deception game.

"This is a great setup," Officer Denver continued. "Have you lived in Seattle long?"

Pound. Pound. Pound. "Uh, I'm actually relatively new to the area. I moved here from the East Coast." Not *exactly* a lie.

Officer Barkman glanced around the shop. "You must have been doing pretty well out there to be able to move and buy a store like this."

"You know, I, uh, got lucky in the stock market." Close. She had gotten lucky in the spy market. Right?

Officer Denver took a step closer. He was a hottie, no doubt. Blond hair, blue eyes, nice crisp uniform. "If you're new in town, maybe you'd like to get to know a strong young officer of the law who can show you all the best spots."

She wanted to say, "Yes, I would love a personalized tour of the greater Seattle metropolitan area." But hanging out with the fuzz would complicate matters beyond belief. And the mission came first. *That* fact had been driven home when she had resisted calling her parents this afternoon. Nonetheless, she needed to keep these guys on her good side.

"I would love to go out with you," she responded flirtatiously. "But I moved here to be closer to my boyfriend . . . and I don't think he would approve."

Officer Denver bowed. "Understood. But if you two call it quits, look me up."

Caylin nodded. "You can count on it." She twirled a piece of her newly red hair and smiled in a way that she knew highlighted her dimple.

"Make sure you lock the doors at night," Officer Barkman warned. "There are some pretty unsavory characters wandering around these days."

Again Caylin smiled her dumb redhead smile. "Will do. Thanks for the heads up."

The policemen ambled out of the store, probably in search of doughnuts and coffee. Caylin collapsed against the counter, limp with relief. Her disguise was a success. If two cops hadn't discerned her true identity, who would?

Jo stuck out a hip and tried to look uninterested in the conversation taking place between Rosebud and his cohort. "What can I get for you guys?" she asked, order pad at the ready.

Rosebud was staring at the chalkboard menu hanging over the counter. "I'll have an American coffee. Black." His eyes traveled from the menu to Jo's legs to Jo's face.

"Gotcha." Jo wrote down the order, keeping her face averted from Rosebud's dark eyes. Being recognized at this point could lead to some oh-so-ugly repercussions.

She turned to Rosebud's companion, who vaguely resembled a puppy in a shop window—soft, cuddly, and hopeful. "What can I get for you?"

"Café au lait, please," the guy responded politely. Jo noted a point in his favor. He wasn't staring at her chest *or* her legs. "Be right back with those, boys. Sit tight." Jo walked quickly back to the counter and handed her order to Doris, who was taking care of the coffee fixings.

So. Everything was fine. Rosebud hadn't recognized her. He'd been staring, sure, but lots of guys stared at Jo. The disguise was a go. She was, for the moment, safe.

"Were they nice?" Doris asked.

Jo shrugged. "I've met better." But I've never met worse, she thought.

Doris glanced back at the table. "Maybe you've met better, but it looks like they haven't."

Don't tell me, Jo thought. She looked back at the table. Oh, no. Rosebud and Mr. X had their heads bent close together, and they were most definitely gazing in her direction. And they were talking. Jo's stomach dropped into her carefully pedicured toes.

"Order up!" Doris announced. She placed the coffees on Jo's tray.

Back into the rats' nest. Jo carried the tray to the small table and set down the orders. "Here you go, guys. Happy java." She turned to go.

"Wait!" Rosebud put a restraining hand on Jo's wrist. "Have we met somewhere before?"

Jo looked him straight in the eyes. What choice did she have? Rosebud's dark gaze bored into hers with an intensity that she might have found mesmerizing under different circumstances.

Yeah, we met, she answered silently. You were wishing you could make it out of that giant pond in time to blow off the heads of me and my friends. Probably not the best approach.

Just the sound of Rosebud's voice made her skin crawl, but Jo clicked into Spy Girl mode and did what she had to do. She flashed him a dazzling I-want-to-go-on-a-date-with-you-more-than-I-want-to-do-anything-in-the-world smile.

"I wish," she replied. Jo gripped her tray with both hands and prayed the floor of Mega Mocha would open up and swallow her whole.

"I *know* we've met," Rosebud insisted. "Do you hang out at Murray's Bar at the pier?"

Proceed with caution, Carreras, Jo told herself. "I don't think so," she said in a breathy voice. "I, uh, don't go out much. I, um, spend most of my free time taking care of my sick aunt Rose." Rose?

Yikes! She couldn't believe she'd used that word!

Rosebud continued to stare, unflinching. "It'll come to me, sweetie. I never forget a face."

Pound. Pound. "Well, I'm sure I could never forget *your* face, either . . . handsome." Oh, the things a girl had to say to get by in this big, bad world. "I'd love to stay and chat, but the crowds are demanding their caffeine."

Holding her tray in a strategic location, Jo grabbed her Great Lash cam from the pocket of her apron with her free hand. She was still within so-called shooting range, just feet from the table.

"You all enjoy that coffee . . . and the view," she said with a lilt. Ugh. Gross flirting made a chick feel dirty.

While Rosebud got visually reacquainted with her legs, she tilted the tiny camera toward his face. Snap. She tilted it toward Mr. X. Snap. Now they were captured on film. Finally. Jo had done something covert.

She raced back to the counter, gasping for breath. Inhale. Exhale. For the next fifteen minutes Jo paid very little attention to her other customers and watched Rosebud and Mr. X in the least conspicuous manner possible. Nothing very remarkable happened—well, almost nothing. In a move so swift that Jo wondered if she had imagined it, Rosebud handed Mr. X a piece of what looked like notebook paper. Interesting—perhaps. At last the guys got up to split.

Rosebud caught her watching him and waved.

"See you tomorrow?" he asked with a wink.

Jo gave him double-dimple action. "Maybe."

"Ooh, he has a *thing* for you," Doris whispered. "Their eyes met across the crowded cafe—it was love at first sight. . . ."

Just as long as he doesn't have it *in* for me, Jo thought as she felt the walls of the cafe closing in on her. The mission was getting more complicated and more dangerous by the hour.

Jo patted the mascara cam in her apron pocket for comfort. She was a Spy Girl. Danger was a major ingredient in her new life. She just didn't want tragedy spilling into the mix.

"Should I wear my khakis or the pale pink midi-skirt?" Theresa asked Caylin and Jo on Tuesday night. She held up both items of clothing for their inspection.

Jo slid off the bed and circled the garments in question. "Are we going for sexpot or good girl?"

Sexpot. Hmmm. Theresa shrugged. "Somewhere in between." She threw the pink midi aside. Definitely too good girl.

Caylin walked to Theresa's closet and pulled out an ice blue silk shirt. "Wear Jo's black leather pants with this blouse," she suggested. "And you can top off the whole thing with some black platform tennis shoes."

"Black leather pants?" Theresa was horrified. She regarded the proposed outfit carefully. "Well . . . maybe . . ."

Jo flopped onto Theresa's bed. "Are we going to keep discussing Theresa's wardrobe for her date—which supposedly isn't a *real* date but merely a fact-finding mission—or are we going to freak over my encounter with Rosebud?"

Theresa guiltily set aside the black pants. Jo was right. The mission was the most important thing in her life right now. "So he recognized you? Rosebud?"

Jo nodded. "He knew I looked familiar . . . he just didn't know *why*." She ran a hand through her hair. "Thank goodness for my skunk locks. I think these streaks saved my butt."

"Tell us about the guy Rosebud was with," Caylin said. "What did he look like?"

"He was young, cute, etc., etc. At one point Rosebud handed the guy a piece of notebook paper, but I couldn't get close enough to find out what was written on it." She sat up and snapped her fingers. "Duh! I *totally* forgot I took pictures of the dudes with my mascara cam. You girls can see Mr. X for yourselves."

"Let's waste no time, Spy Girls," Caylin said. "Hey, *Tessa*, can you spare a few moments before your tête-à-tête to scan in the pics?"

"Of course." Theresa slipped into the chair in front of her laptop and booted up. "You know, Brad really *is* going to be a good info source—I think."

"Yeah, yeah. Computer geeks are notorious for helping out international spies with dangerous missions," Caylin said. "Happens all the time."

"Enough!" Theresa took the lash cam from Jo's outstretched hand and hooked it up to the computer. "In case you two wonder twins hadn't noticed, *this* computer geek has done plenty on the international spy circuit."

"Touché!" Jo called. "How did the pics turn out?"

"Hold on . . . I'll tell you in a second." Theresa watched as the digital photos appeared on-screen. "Oh my . . ."

Jo and Caylin peered over Theresa's shoulder. "That's Rosebud, all right," Caylin commented. "I'd recognize those coal black eyes anywhere."

"But . . . but . . ." Theresa couldn't get the words out.

Jo waved a hand in front of Theresa's face. "What?"

"That's Brad!" she finally squeaked. "The other guy is *my* Brad."

"Your nerd?" Caylin asked. "*He's* the guy who was meeting with Rosebud?"

Theresa nodded. "Yeah . . . that's him." No wonder Brad hadn't been able to go to lunch with her this afternoon. When he'd said "appointment," she'd assumed it was with a doctor or a dentist. Not this. *Anything* but this.

"Does anyone know how 'The Funeral March' goes?" Jo asked. "I think we're going to need it."

Theresa shook her head. "Something isn't right. I *know* Brad is a good guy. I can feel it."

"You feel *lust*," Jo said. "If the geek—albeit *cute* geek—is meeting with Rosebud, then he's definitely involved in the No Good."

"Whether he's good or bad, this new development poses some interesting possibilities." Caylin twirled a strand of her red hair around a finger and stared thoughtfully at the digital photos.

"Please expound," Theresa said. "Right now I'm willing to try anything to get to the bottom of this nightmare."

"You can kill Brad with kindness . . . so to speak," Caylin explained. "If he really is one of the bad dudes, maybe you can coax him into giving you key data."

"And if he isn't, then I can grill him for information about Rosebud," Theresa concluded.

"Exactly."

Theresa pushed out the desk chair and walked back to the closet. "In that case, I'd better get ready for my date." She pulled her platform tennis shoes out of the closet. "I'm just glad Brad decided we should meet later in the evening. If we had left from work like we planned . . ."

"We never would have known that Brad might be a psycho," Jo finished the thought. "Meanwhile Caylin and I better put on our computer geek duds, too. We'll back you up all the way."

Theresa pulled on the silk blouse. "Phew! I didn't want to ask . . ."

"But it's always nice to have an extra Spy Girl or two around when you're getting smoochie with a guy who might be planning to out you to Rosebud."

"You read my mind." Theresa laughed. Now. She was going to have to think about makeup. Evil or not, Brad deserved at least a little lip gloss. Cherry? Or strawberry? Hmmm . . .

* * *

"Is this place for real?" Caylin asked Jo on Tuesday night. "I feel like I've just walked into an episode of *Star Trek: The Next Generation.*"

"American culture has certainly taken a turn toward the weird," Jo agreed. The pair had followed Brad and Theresa to Arcadia, a twenty-four-hour, mall-sized, high-tech, video/virtual reality arcade. There were games everywhere, and the place was packed.

"How long are we going to have to sit in this virtual reality booth?" Caylin asked. "I'm getting a headache."

Jo negotiated her virtual car around a tight curve on a virtual freeway. "This is a perfect spot for the Rosebud Watch," she pointed out. "Besides, I'm having fun."

Caylin stuck her head out of the booth. "I don't think he's here. The scumbag would totally stick out in a place like this." She paused. "However, I think we're being checked out by two semihottie nerds who are playing the Ninja game."

"You don't say?" Jo's virtual Mercedes convertible spun out of control and she crashed. "Ouch." *Game Over* flashed mercilessly across the large screen in front of her. "Okay, okay, I can take a hint."

"Let's canvas the area for Rosebud," Caylin suggested. "Maybe he's hiding in one of the life-sized virtual boxing games." She slid out of her seat and stretched. Whew. No wonder people were drawn here. This was some intense stuff. Theresa was probably loving every second of it.

"Good plan. But we've got to keep a low profile," Jo replied as she stepped out of the machine. "Even if Rosebud is hiding in his lair tonight, I don't want the Bradster to get a gander of me."

The girls circled the area surrounding Brad and Theresa, who seemed engrossed in a game of electronic chess. They looked into every virtual reality booth, behind every video game, and even kept a short post next to the door of the men's bathroom. Nothing.

"I don't think Rosebud is here," Jo concluded. "We'd be able to sense his evil presence."

Caylin nodded. "I'm inclined to agree. I mean, what kind of malicious plan could be afoot for the night? I don't know too many crooks who warm up for illegal activity with a relaxing game of chess."

Jo giggled. "Theresa actually looks like she's having *fun*."

Caylin followed Jo's gaze. Theresa was laughing, her lip gloss shining effectively in Arcadia's techno lighting. "Different strokes."

"Well, remind *me* never to consent to a date with a computer geek," Jo said. "I prefer candlelight and slow jams."

Caylin sighed softly. At this rate it seemed unlikely that *any* of the Spy Girls *ever* was going to be romanced in a serious way. The idea of getting into a relationship was out of the question. Too bad. Caylin remembered what it was like to have a boyfriend—and she missed it.

* * *

"Sorry about that last checkmate," Theresa said as she climbed into a virtual reality game that promised to send her to the moon.

"Hey, I can take being beat four games in a row," he responded, taking a seat close beside her. "I'm humbled . . . but very impressed."

"I, uh, play a lot of computer chess," Theresa explained as she put on the provided VR headgear. She knew most guys wouldn't find that statement to be terribly enticing, but Brad wasn't like most guys.

"Cool." Brad dropped several tokens into the slot and plunked on the headgear, and the ride to the moon began.

Theresa stared in awe as she flew through virtual outer space. She felt herself slipping into another state of being. She was no longer Tessa Somerset; she wasn't even Theresa Hearth anymore. She was Neil Armstrong, headed for that great big ball of cream cheese in the sky.

"This is awesome," Theresa said. "I can't wait to say, 'The *Eagle* has landed.'"

"Me neither," Brad agreed. He looked away from the screen and aimed his goggles in Theresa's direction. "You know, you're an amazing person, Tessa." Brad's voice was warm and sincere. "Most girls would think this kind of stuff is stupid."

Theresa navigated the spacecraft toward the cratered surface of the moon. "Are you kidding? I'm in heaven."

No lie there. She *was* having a great time. Brad seemed like such a nice, normal guy. Was it really possible that he was involved with Rosebud?

Theresa racked her brain for an alternate explanation for his presence at Mega Mocha today. Maybe Rosebud was after him. Yeah, that had to be it. Rosebud had Brad pegged as a gullible guy who, with a little threatening and/or blackmail, would help him extract the code. That had to be it.

They were getting closer and closer to the moon. Now was the time to pry Brad for Rosebud info. He was totally entranced by the screen in front of them. Too entranced to be suspicious, hopefully.

"So there must be some pretty crazy characters hanging around FutureWorks." It was a statement, not a question.

"Yeah, I guess." Brad continued guiding them toward the moon's surface.

"Does anyone ever, like, try to take advantage of your vast knowledge of mainframes?" Theresa asked. "I mean, people try to do some pretty insane stuff with the Internet."

"The *Eagle* has landed!" Brad shouted.

Oops. She had missed her line. Oh, well.

"You know, people stealing credit card numbers and stuff right off the web." She negotiated her virtual self out of the space shuttle and took a step onto the moon. Unreal!

Brad took off his headgear. "Tell you what, Tessa. Let's split," he suggested. "I want to show you something."

"But we're still on the moon." And I'm not done pumping you for information, she added silently.

"There's not much to see. Just a lot of rocks and dust." He stepped out of the booth and held out a hand.

She slipped off her headgear and took Brad's hand. "Where are we going?"

"Like I told you yesterday, it's a surprise." Brad gently placed his hand on the small of her back and guided her toward the huge red exit sign over one of the doors.

Theresa glanced surreptitiously over one shoulder. She couldn't see Jo and Caylin. But she was sure they would follow at a safe distance. And if they somehow got separated, then Theresa was confident she could handle Brad by herself. It wouldn't be *that* hard, would it?

"Say, 'supermodel,'" Jo cheered as the camera in the tiny photo booth clicked.

"Supermodel!" Caylin yelled. She stuck out her tongue and crossed her eyes. "Say, 'Uncle Sam'!"

"Uncle Sam!" Jo pursed her lips and tried to look semiseductive. The camera clicked again. "I love these booths."

Bored by watching the tedious progress of Brad and Theresa's fourth game of chess, Jo and Caylin had decided to explore the rest of Arcadia just in case Rosebud was hiding out in some heretofore undiscovered location. They hadn't found the tattooed one, but they *had* found a vintage, coin-operated photo booth. It proved the ideal tool for capturing their new makeovers on film for posterity.

"Too bad Theresa isn't with us," Caylin said. "It

could have been a full-on Spy Girls photo session."

"Theresa! When was the last time we checked on her and the 'meister?" Even as she posed the question, Jo knew the answer.

Too long.

The girls stared at each other as the camera snapped one more time. "Let's go!" they chorused.

They more or less fell out of the booth and raced to the section of the arcade that housed the electronic chessboards. Nothing. No one. Nada.

"They're not there," Jo said, stating the obvious. She looked wildly around the large arcade. By now the crowd had thinned out. The place was nearly empty, and there was no sign of Theresa or Brad.

"She's gone!" Caylin shrieked. Her face turned a peculiar shade that was somewhere between mustard yellow and pea green. "But we're not alone."

"Huh?" Jo was still scanning the room for a sign of Theresa's pale blue shirt.

"I just saw Rosebud—and he saw me." Caylin's voice was trembling as she spoke.

"Three, two, one, we're *outta* here!" Jo tugged on Caylin's arm and the girls fled.

"Now the real fun begins," Brad said as he led Theresa down a dark Seattle block.

"I'm intrigued." Theresa glanced around, taking in the sights. Huh. There was Mega Mocha. And now they were at the corner of Fleet Street.

"Is it my imagination, or are we walking to FutureWorks?" Theresa asked.

"You guessed it," Brad answered with a grin.

"Wow, you're a real romantic," Theresa joked. "We're going back to work for our first date?" But inside, she was shaking with a combo of excitement and nervousness. Was it possible that Brad was going to lead her straight to the code? It was. Unfortunately she couldn't ignore the fact that Brad could also be leading her straight to Rosebud and the barrel of a gun.

"I may not be great on the flowers and candy front, but I'm going to give you a night to remember," Brad said. "I'm going to show you what FutureWorks is *really* about."

Perfect, she thought. That was exactly what she wanted to hear. "I can't wait." And she meant that literally. The global economy was at stake.

"Take this," Brad said.

Theresa glanced at a rectangular piece of laminated plastic Brad had handed to her. Whoa. It was a fake security pass—complete with her photo! Okay, that explained the digital candid. But what was he up to? "Care to explain?" she asked.

He shook his head. "You'll just have to trust me."

At this point Theresa didn't trust *anyone.* Good thing Jo and Caylin were close behind. At least, she *assumed* they were.

"You're an expert," Theresa exclaimed, closely examining the pass. "This looks like the real deal."

Brad put his arm around her shoulders and squeezed. "I'm full of surprises, Tessa."

So am I, Theresa answered silently. So am I.

Run!" Caylin yelled. "Run!" She could almost feel Rosebud's breath on the back of her neck as she raced through Arcadia.

"I *am* running," Jo panted. "But he's still after us."

Caylin pushed through a door marked No Entry and yanked Jo inside. They stopped in their tracks and looked around. Where were they? The room was dark and huge, with high ceilings. People wearing neon jerseys raced from side to side. Techno music blasted at an ear-shattering level.

"It's laser tag!" Jo said. "Let's find another way out!"

The girls joined hands and sprinted across the room. "Where's the exit?" Caylin shouted. She saw stairs and small *American Gladiator*–style barricades, but no other doors.

"I don't know—we just got more company!" Jo yelled over the music. Behind them Rosebud had slipped inside.

"I'm It!" Rosebud bellowed. "And you two are dead!"

Jo and Caylin ran behind an enormous speaker and squatted close to the floor. "There's got to be another exit!" Jo cried.

"I know!" Caylin shouted. "But it's so dark in here, I can't see anything!"

As Caylin's eyes adjusted to the dark room she peered out from behind the speaker. On the far side of the room she spotted a long, narrow staircase. She nudged Jo, pointing.

"Take the stairs!" Caylin screamed.

The girls darted out and raced across the room. They tripped up the steps two at a time. At the top Caylin realized they were on some kind of spectators' deck. She peered over the ledge. "Where is he?"

Gasping for breath, Jo staggered to Caylin's side. "There he is! Down there!" She pointed toward the laser tag floor. Yes! Rosebud was surrounded by a dozen angry nerds.

"Get off the floor, dude!" one of them yelled. "You're not in the game!"

"Beam him!" someone else shouted.

"I think that's our cue!" Caylin squinted and noticed a door at the end of the corridor marked exit. "Jo! This way!"

Jo and Caylin ran down the spectators' platform and burst through the door. "We're safe!" Jo declared. They were in the parking lot of Arcadia, just steps away from their bus stop.

Caylin leaned against the side of the building, panting. "We may be safe, but we're stupid."

"Why? I mean, aside from the fact that we lost Theresa and Brad and almost got axed by Rosebud." She was holding her sides and blowing sweaty strands of hair off her forehead.

"The pictures," Caylin said flatly. "We forgot the pictures."

"Are we going where I think we're going?" Theresa asked, struggling to keep the excitement out of her voice.

Brad held Theresa's hand as they walked down a long, empty corridor on the second floor of FutureWorks. "Where do you think we're going?" he asked.

"The Monkey Room." She was almost breathless at the thought. The Monkey Room. He might as well have told her he was taking her to Willie Wonka's chocolate factory. This was her golden ticket.

"Yep." Brad grinned proudly. "Impressed?"

"I'm in awe," Theresa responded. "How are we going to get in?"

"You'll see." Brad pulled Theresa to a stop in front of the security desk outside FutureWorks' center of operations. There were two guards on duty. One was deep into the latest issue of the *National Enquirer*. The other was dozing in front of a tiny black-and-white television set.

Well. Lax security or not, Jo and Caylin wouldn't be able to scam their way past the tank-proof metal door blocking Theresa's path. If they were still tailing her at all, that is. Theresa was on her own . . . which was fine. Fine. Really.

"Hey, guys," Brad said casually to the rent-a-cops. "We're here for a virus check. The boss said there might be a glitch."

Security guard number one looked up from an article about aliens landing at the Mall of America. "Darn machines. We were better off without 'em."

Brad flashed his security pass, then indicated that Theresa should do the same. She held up her fake pass for inspection, but the guard barely gave it a glance. "Don't electrocute yourselves in there," he said. Then he pushed a small red button. And the door opened.

Brad clasped Theresa's hand and led her through. "This is it," she breathed. "This is the Monkey Room." Behind them the door closed with a soft whoosh. "I can't believe how easy it was to get inside."

"With the right tools, a souped-up PC, and a killer laser printer, *anything* is easy," Brad said proudly. "I got in here for the first time a month ago."

Theresa whistled softly. "This place is . . . incredible." And it was. They had entered what appeared to be a hermetically sealed chamber in which computers were the only decor. The floors were black marble, the walls hospital white. Everywhere Theresa looked, there was some kind of computer, monitor, or modem. On the wall were giant television screens, each of which showed a different site on the Internet. The place was like something out of a high-tech sci-fi movie. Watch out, James Cameron!

"We could do anything from here," Brad said, sitting down in front of one of the computers. "The hard drive of this baby feeds right into the

Internet's mainframe. The information we could access is mind-boggling."

Theresa stood behind him, staring at the computer monitor. "Have you, like, tried to do . . . anything?"

Brad shrugged. "I've done a little hacking . . . nothing major so far." He paused. "If you want, I'll do a little sketch of the security blueprints I found. They're pretty radical."

"Great!" The more she knew about FutureWorks security, the better.

Brad pulled out a piece of notebook paper from the pocket of his khaki pants. Bells went off in Theresa's head as she stared at it. Brad was smoothing out the blank side of the paper, but Theresa was dying to see what was written on its reverse. "Hey, can I take a look at that?" she asked.

"Sure, Tessa. Whatever you want." Brad handed her the paper. "It's just some directions to some kind of game this guy gave me. He said I might find it interesting."

Theresa stared at the note, then pinched herself—hard—on the arm. This was insanity. Written on the simple piece of notebook paper was everything Theresa would need in order to get the code. Sure, she'd have to do some pretty intense work, but the key parts were laid out right in front of her eyes.

"These are instructions," Theresa said. Should she say more? Biting her lip, Theresa decided to go for it. "They're instructions that could lead us to an extremely powerful code . . . or something."

"Wow." Brad stared at the writing on the page. "What do you want to do with it?"

Now *there* was a dumb question. "Let's follow the instructions," Theresa suggested excitedly. Was Brad really as clueless as he appeared? Or was he setting her up?

"I don't know. . . ." Brad's voice trailed off. "Those are some pretty intricate steps. I don't even know if I could make the transition from one instruction to the next."

This was the moment of truth. If Brad was playing dumb, it meant that there was a possibility that this whole situation had been engineered to Get Her. Maybe she would follow these instructions only to set off some kind of doomsday device that would blow her to tiny bits. But Brad was standing right next to her. Any harm she suffered would be suffered by him as well. Besides, time was running out. She had to go for it.

"I'll do it." Theresa slid into a chair in front of the computer. "Just get me a blank disk, and I'll take care of the rest."

Theresa's palms were sweating as she followed the first instruction. If all went according to plan, half an hour from now she would be able to say, "Mission accomplished."

"They probably went for a cup of coffee or something to eat," Caylin speculated. She was sipping a cup of lemon herbal tea and lounging on the leather sofa in a pair of sweats and soft cotton flannel. "Or maybe Brad wanted to show Theresa an all-night computer software shop."

"Yeah . . . I'm sure they're engaged in some perfectly harmless activity," Jo agreed. "Pretty soon Theresa will waltz in here all starry-eyed over the cyberkiss they shared." She stuffed half a sprinkled doughnut into her mouth.

"Right." So why did Caylin have that queasy feeling that usually meant trouble?

"Let's watch some tube," Jo suggested. "There's nothing like a bad sitcom to take your mind off body-art-ridden psychopaths."

Caylin glanced at her watch. "I'd love to spend a half hour watching the latest and lamest in prime time, but I think we'd better check out the news."

Jo sighed. "No rest for the weary." But she switched on the local news, anyway.

". . . And this just in from the AP," a perky blond who had had one too many nose jobs trilled. "Brazen criminals change their appearances and smile for the camera!"

The anchorwoman's button nose was replaced with photographs of Jo and Caylin, resplendent in their new hair and makeup.

"No!" Caylin wailed. "Don't even tell me."

"Our quick pics," Jo stated. "The press got the prints from our impromptu photo session."

"How?" Caylin wondered, transfixed by the television screen. "I mean, we took those, like, an hour ago. How could the media possibly have gotten ahold of them?"

"Rosebud." Jo tossed the remote control at the television set and groaned. "He knew we were in the photo booth the whole time. And once we escaped, he went back and got the pictures."

"He's determined to get us arrested for that limo driver's murder," Caylin said. "And he's doing a pretty good job of it."

"That lout thinks he can frame us, get the code, and flee for who-knows-where with a Swiss bank account stuffed with zillions." Jo's voice was sad, resigned.

"That's what he *thinks*," Caylin growled, incensed. "But he doesn't know who he's dealing with."

Instantly Jo perked up. "Yeah . . . he doesn't know who he's dealing with!"

Caylin jabbed a finger toward the TV set. "We're the Spy Girls! There's no way we're letting him get away with that kind of bull."

"You said it, sister!" Jo jumped up, rallying. "Rosebud, prepare for jail! We're going to get you!"

Caylin hopped off the couch. There was a lot of thinking to do. But before they could devise a plan, they needed one very important Spy Girl. Theresa. Caylin just hoped that Theresa was somewhere safe and happily hacking, not getting *hacked up.*

Forty minutes after sitting down in front of the computer, Theresa was sweating. Even with instructions she had to use one hundred percent of her brainpower to extract the code from the system. And now, as she pressed enter, she was prepared to see the end of the rainbow right on the monitor of the supercomputer.

"Enter," she whispered. The screen went black. "Dang!" She had failed. Theresa dropped her head in her hands and resisted the urge to cry.

Behind her Brad placed a gentle hand on her shoulder. "Wait—look!"

Theresa glanced back at the screen. Finally! There was the code—the be-all and end-all of this seemingly ill-fated mission—flashing right in front of her eyes. Yes!

Despair vanished and was quickly replaced with an intense rush of adrenaline. Theresa tapped the keyboard lightning quick, working deftly to store the code on disk. "Now it's time to say, 'bye-bye,'" she told the computer softly, her finger poised over the key that would extract the last little bit of information pertaining to the code from the mainframe forever. "But first, a word from our sponsors." How could she resist? By the time one of the bad guys got to her personal greeting, she would be *long* gone.

> *So long, suckers!*
> *You* won't *be laughing all the way to the bank!*
> *Nyeah-nyeah!*

Theresa saved the message on the computer, did one last check to assure herself that all useful information had been removed from the mainframe, then popped out the disk. *Finit.* She held out the disk for Brad's inspection. "Here it is. The key to the world's economy."

Brad took a couple of steps backward. "I don't think I want to be anywhere near that thing. It's, like, radiating power or something."

"I'll keep it," Theresa offered. Was this another trap? If so, Theresa was beyond caring. There was no way she wanted to let go of this disk no matter *what* travails she'd have to face. "Let's book."

"Wait—we've got one more stop," Brad told her.

Theresa followed Brad out of the Monkey Room, past the guards, and into the elevators, feeling increasingly nervous. What the heck was going on? Why was he taking her to the thirtieth floor?

"I'm stumped," Theresa said as she trailed Brad out of the elevator and down the hall to their shared cubicle. "Why are we back at our desks?" She had just experienced the most exciting hour of her life, and she was anxious to get back to HQ to fill in Jo and Caylin on the details. Plus she wanted to get the disk to safety ASAP.

"Getting into the Monkey Room is only step one," Brad explained calmly. "Now we have to make sure that the head cheeses never know we invaded their precious nerve center."

"This is yet another surprise, I take it," Theresa said, grinning at Brad. Why were his hazel eyes so sincere? Their warmth made it extremely difficult for her to maintain a healthy Spy Girl distance.

Brad nodded as he booted up his computer. "We've got to erase the digital security photos that were taken of us on our way in and out of the Monkey Room."

The guy thought of everything. Theresa had been *more* than satisfied with getting the code. But of course Brad was right . . . there was no doubt that whoever was in charge of Operation Money Grab paid close attention to who entered and exited the center of operations. She watched Brad's computer machinations, impressed.

"Like so. And so. And so." The digital photos that had filled Brad's monitor moments ago disappeared. "We're now nonpeople," Brad explained. "According to any record—official or unofficial—we never dropped by Ye Olde Monkey Room."

Theresa stared at Brad. Was this dude for real? He had given her a road map to the code. It was almost as if he had *wanted* her to find the answers she was looking for. Victor had tried to help, but he'd done little more than give her a few cryptic tips and let her off early from work when she needed to attend an emergency conference. But Brad . . . he had been an angel.

Hmmm. Could Brad actually be working for The Tower? Was it possible that he had been sent to meet up with Rosebud and garner information about the code *and* the frame-up? Truth be told, Theresa didn't know all that much about the guy. And it would be just like The Tower to install another agent without revealing it. They were masters of secrecy. Heck . . . the theory was worth a shot.

"Do you do a lot of, uh, covert computer work?" Theresa asked pointedly. "I mean, besides this FutureWorks stuff?"

"Um . . . one time I hacked into the Internet and read my older brother's e-mail," Brad answered. "But that was because I was really mad at him."

He wasn't biting. "Do you like, uh, James Bond movies?" Theresa asked. "I mean, I love all that *spy* stuff. The gadgets, the heroism, the secrecy—"

Brad snorted. "Are you *joking?* That stuff is *totally* unrealistic. Spies went out with the end of the cold war. Everyone knows that."

"Right. Right." Theresa felt her face turning crimson. Okay. Brad wasn't a Tower employee. That fact was all too clear. "It's just that I think you would make a great undercover agent. You're so smart and, like, covert."

"Really? You think so?" Brad switched off his computer and took a step toward Theresa. "I've never had anyone tell me I'd be a great spy before. . . ."

His voice was soft, gravelly, mesmerizing. Brad was just inches from her now. And he was leaning closer and closer. Theresa closed her eyes. For one minute she was going to allow herself to be a girl, minus the "spy" she usually put in front of that particular label. She *was* human—code or no code.

A moment later Brad's lips touched hers. And

Theresa forgot all about the code, the Monkey Room, and Rosebud. For now she was *really* enjoying being kissed.

"This is too much," Uncle Sam said over the speakerphone, his voice dark. "The Tower has never suffered such overt humiliation." For several long seconds the only sound in the room was that of Uncle Sam's heavy breathing. And then he spoke. "This mission is over. I want you out of Seattle at the crack of dawn."

Calling Uncle Sam had seemed like a good idea a few minutes ago. Emergency contact with The Tower usually resulted in at least one helpful hint. But Jo was beginning to question the wisdom of their decision.

"No way!" Jo exclaimed. "We can't abandon the mission."

Maybe they *shouldn't* have told Uncle Sam about the quick pics from Arcadia. After she and Caylin had taken turns describing the latest catastrophic sequence of events, Uncle Sam had exploded. And things were going from bad to worse. To worst.

"Besides, Theresa is out gathering info as we speak!" Caylin insisted. "We can't quit now."

"Give us a break, Jo," Uncle Sam snapped. "You and Caylin are having a high old time giving each other makeovers—and recording the whole thing for the world to see, no less."

"But Theresa—," Caylin interrupted.

"Theresa is out on a date," Uncle Sam said. "Victor told me all about it. You three are useless."

"No, we're not!" Jo shouted. "We can complete this mission. I know we can!" She took a deep breath and struggled to regain her tenuous grip on calm. "We've just hit a few bumps in the road."

"This mission is over," Uncle Sam repeated flatly. "And so are the Spy Girls."

Theresa slipped her arms around Brad's waist as he pulled her closer. His lips were soft and warm and absolutely thrilling. Theresa melted into the kiss, savoring every moment.

Beep. Beep. Beep.

Dang. An annoying sound was invading the purity of her make-out session.

Beep. Beep. Beep.

Brad pulled away. "Is that your pager, Tessa?"

"Tessa?" Double oops. One little kiss shouldn't have made her forget her alias. "I mean, yeah. Yes!" She stepped out of Brad's arms and dug her pager out of the small handbag she had brought on the date. The message on the beeper was clear: *911.* So much for smooching. She had to get back to HQ double-quick.

"Uh-oh, I gotta leave," Theresa told Brad.

"Why?" Brad was staring at her intently, arousing suspicion once again.

"It's my, uh, cat again. My roommate and I have a special cat-alert code." Theresa slipped on her jacket and smiled ruefully at Brad. "Sorry to kiss and run . . ." And she was even sorrier that she wouldn't be seeing him again. By this time tomorrow she would be halfway across the country.

"I'll walk you out," Brad offered, holding out his arm to Theresa.

"Thank you, kind sir."

Theresa followed Brad out of the office, thinking about their date from start to finish. The guy was too sweet to be evil. There was just no way that Brad was anything but a cute, semiclueless, but very endearing computer geek who was being used by Rosebud as some kind of weird pawn.

The trip to the ground floor of FutureWorks passed in a blur. Now that Theresa had recovered from Brad's spine-tingling kiss, her thoughts had turned to Jo and Caylin. What was the emergency? Cops? Rosebud? Well, whatever the problem was, they would handle it. Now that Theresa had possession of the mission-completing information, they were home free.

Theresa trailed Brad out of the building, admiring the way his strong, broad back moved. It was too bad that ending the mission meant ending her romantic dalliance, but such was the life of a Spy Girl.

"Hello, kids." A dark figure stepped out of the shadows, blocking Brad and Theresa's path. "Nice evening, isn't it?"

A dangerous chill traveled down the length of Theresa's spine—significantly *less* pleasant than the chill she had felt in Brad's arms. Even in the dim light of the street she recognized Rosebud's face. There was no doubt that if he turned around, she would see the small, red tattoo on the back of his neck.

"What do you want?" Brad asked. "We were just leaving."

Rosebud sneered. "I want the disk, Brad." He paused, looking from Theresa to Brad to Theresa. "I believe you have it. And I want it now."

Brad stepped forward, blocking Theresa from Rosebud's view. "I don't have any disk, Simon," he said. "I don't know what you're talking about."

Rosebud laughed. "Yeah, right. There's no way you resisted going into the Monkey Room with that info I gave you today, geek. Why else would you be here late at night?"

"Tessa left her house keys in the office," Brad said. "Now I'd appreciate it if you got out of our way. We have a late date with a cat named Fluffy."

Theresa's heart was hammering in her chest. Brad certainly didn't appear to be in cahoots with Rosebud. And Rosebud didn't even seem to know who she was. She planned to keep it that way.

Moving as if to take off her jacket, Theresa surreptitiously slid the disk into the waistband of her black pants. She would die before she gave it up to Rosebud.

"Trying to impress your girlfriend by showing her your big, bad computer skills, Bradley?" Rosebud chided. "I'm sure watching you hack got her all hot and bothered."

"Leave Tessa out of this," Brad said. "Unless you want me to put my fist in your ugly face."

This encounter was *not* going smoothly. Theresa was going to keep her mouth shut, bide her time, and bolt. She hated to leave Brad on his own, but the entire world economy was at stake.

Ten, nine, eight, seven, *zero.* Theresa made a move to sprint.

Rosebud stepped in front of her. "You're not going anywhere, sweetheart. Neither of you is going anywhere until I get my hands on that disk." He pulled a small handgun out of the pocket of his trench coat. "Now get moving. We're all going back to work."

Going inside isn't an option, Theresa realized. This was her only opportunity to get away, and she was going to seize it—gun or no gun. Theresa faked right, then ran. But before she got twenty feet away, Theresa felt the heavy blow of a cold, blunt object against the side of her head.

She crumpled to the sidewalk. Black dots floated before her eyes. A moment later the street seemed to be retreating farther and farther into the distance. And then her world faded to black.

"Why hasn't she responded to our page?" Jo shouted. "She knows a 911 means circumstances aren't just sticky, they're downright dire."

"Well, she didn't answer the beep the other night," Caylin pointed out. "Maybe she just didn't think there was anything that could be important enough to take her away from her date." Caylin *wished* she believed a word of what she had just said. In truth, she was as panicked as Jo.

"Something is wrong," Jo said. "Something went seriously amiss, and Theresa needs our help."

Caylin had to agree. Drastic action was in order. But what? "We can't call Uncle Sam."

Jo snorted. "Ah, no. That would be, like, the worst idea in the universe."

Caylin stared into space, concentrating. Then she snapped her fingers. "Let's call Vince or Victor or whatever that Tower agent guy's name is. I'll dial."

Caylin pulled the speakerphone close while Jo went to the kitchen. She grabbed a tiny coded electronic address book—the one that held the direct numbers of all Tower contacts—from behind a flour jar.

Victor picked up on the first ring. "Yes?" Despite the semilate hour, Victor sounded alert and ready for action. Thank goodness.

Caylin briefed him quickly, explaining that she and Jo were the agents working in concert with Theresa, his contact. The more she talked, the more she realized just how dangerous circumstances had become. She and Jo were wanted—makeovers and all—by every police officer in the state, and Theresa was effectively MIA.

"I can see why you girls are worried," Victor said when Caylin paused to breathe. "Clearly we must take steps to find Theresa."

"Yes!" Jo enthused. "Now you're speaking our language."

"I suggest you two meet me in front of FutureWorks as soon as possible," Victor said. "I don't want to go into details, but I have a hunch about what may be holding up your friend."

Hunches were good. Well, they weren't as good as actual concrete information, but Caylin wasn't about to argue. She and Jo were fresh out of ideas. "We'll put together some quick disguises and meet you in twenty minutes," Caylin promised. She hung up the phone.

"Looks like we're going to have to go with the turban and I-wear-my-sunglasses-at-night look," Jo said. "We've gone through everything else."

Caylin nodded. She would be willing to dress up as a Georgia peach if it meant they could complete this mission, redeem themselves, and live to spy another day. "Come on, Mata Hari," she said. "We've got lives to save."

Theresa blinked. She was dimly aware of a dull, throbbing pain in the back of her head. Slowly her surroundings came into focus. She was at her desk, in her chair. No, she wasn't just *in* her chair—she was tied to it! Theresa stared across the small office area and saw that Brad was bound in a similar fashion.

"Tessa?" he whispered. "Are you all right?"

She squeezed her eyes shut for a moment. "Um, aside from the obvious fact that I'm tied to a chair and my head feels like it's been booted up with an infected disk, I'm fine." Waking up a prisoner made her grouchy.

"Shut up!" Rosebud shouted at Theresa. "I'm thinking." He was standing in front of Brad's computer, pounding away at the keys. "It's gone. It's all gone. . . . I knew you extracted the code. I just knew it."

Theresa was beginning to regret the chirpy message she had left in place of the code. Apparently the computers at her and Brad's desks were more powerful than she had realized. Then again, Rosebud *was* the evil genius who had programmed the code in the first place. He didn't even need to go to the Monkey Room to assess the damage Theresa had done earlier.

A moment later the message flashed on the screen.

So long, suckers . . .

She didn't need to read the rest. Rosebud's face had turned a bright, angry red, and his teeth were bared as if he were a bulldog going in for a kill. "Where is it, Bradley?" he growled. "I know you have it. Give it to me. It's *mine.*"

"Wait a minute." Theresa looked away from Rosebud and confronted Brad. "You *knew* he was going to meet us here, didn't you?" she cried. "You're in on this! You had *me* extract the code so that you could give it to him and get off scot-free!"

Brad's eyebrows practically hit the ceiling. "Tessa, what are you—"

"That's it! You're *both* trying to frame me!" Theresa declared. "You wanted in on the deal, Brad, but you didn't want your hands to get dirty."

"*What* deal?" Brad shrieked.

Rosebud banged his fist on the keyboard. "I'd advise you to shut up *right* now, sister, before—"

"How much did he promise you, huh?" Theresa asked Brad. "Half? A quarter? Jeez, one-*sixteenth* of the entire world's economy isn't so bad when you think about it."

Rosebud picked up a monitor and threw it down with a crash. "Shut *up!*" he bellowed.

"How could you set me up, Brad?" Theresa asked tearfully, hoping waterworks would appeal to Brad's overdeveloped sensitive side. "How *could* you?"

Brad shook his head vigorously. "I swear, Tessa. I had no idea that Simon would do something like this. He just said it was a game, that's all. I—I mean, I don't really even know the guy. We met at a computer convention a few weeks ago and . . ."

"Quit your stupid yakking!" Rosebud screamed at Brad. He turned to Theresa with a smug smile. "Allow me to clear things up for you, *Theresa Hearth*. The computer geek never knew what hit him. *He* wasn't the one setting you up. *I* was. In fact, I was setting you *both* up."

Theresa grimaced. Rosebud had known who she was all along. And he had spent the last two days setting this trap . . . one she had walked right into and one that poor, gullible Brad never saw coming. "You're never going to get away with this," she spat out. "The Tower will stop you."

"Theresa?" Brad asked. "Who's Theresa?"

Rosebud backhanded Brad. "Shut up, dweeb." He turned back to Theresa. "I knew I had to get those instructions to you. You're the only person around with the skills to get the code . . . other than me, of course. But there was no way I could extract the code from the mainframe without getting caught—you and your idiot girlfriends were already on my trail. So I passed the info along to the doughboy over here and bingo! Here I am to pluck my code from your hands and be on my merry way. Now hand over the disk."

"I don't have any disk, jerk," Theresa insisted. "The code is gone. Vanished. I deleted it."

"And I happen to know that's impossible," Rosebud countered.

Theresa felt like puking. The code really *couldn't* be deleted, only transferred. Dang. Rosebud was right. He'd caught her. "Whatever," she managed to say. "There's still no disk. Why do you want it, anyway? Isn't the entire world economy supposed to turn over to you, like, by the weekend or something?"

"That's just the problem," Rosebud explained. "It *wasn't* going to turn over to me anymore. Someone else stepped in and decided to cut me out of the equation. So with your help, I'm taking the equation back."

The guy was so smug, so sure that he had won. And here she was, tied to a chair, powerless to stop him from winning this high-stakes game, and only falling deeper into his trap with each second.

Rosebud abandoned the computer. "Now that I've proved that you did in fact get the code, I'm willing to bet the European economy that you've got it hidden on you somewhere." He walked toward Theresa. "I guess I'll just have to do a hands-on search."

Theresa closed her eyes. This was getting worse, worse, worse. She needed an SOS, and she needed it *now.*

"I'm glad you two were able to make it out tonight," Victor said as he hopped out of a taxi in front of FutureWorks. He seemed not to notice that both Jo and Caylin were wearing absurd outfits—pastel turbans, bell-bottoms, and giant sunglasses. They had decided that hiding in plain sight was the best way to avoid a cop confrontation.

"Do you know where she is?" Jo asked breathlessly. "Have you figured it out?"

Victor was calm, cool, and collected. "As I said on the phone, I have a hunch." He opened the door of FutureWorks with his passkey and motioned to the girls. "Let's go in, shall we?"

Energy was seeping out of Jo's pores as she followed Victor into the building. There was an electricity in the air that alerted her to some serious covert activity. Whatever they were about to find was going to make or break the mission.

They were all silent as the elevator rose swiftly and silently to the thirtieth floor. Are you up there, T.? Jo asked silently. Are you in trouble?

"This way, ladies," Victor said as they stepped out of the elevator.

"Let's hope for the best and expect the worst," Caylin suggested as they crept down the long hallway.

"Agreed." Theresa clenched and unclenched her fists, trying in vain to calm her fraying nerves.

"Aha!" Victor said as he turned the last corner. "I knew she was up here!" He stopped short. "But she's not alone."

Caylin and Jo stopped behind Victor. "Theresa!" Jo yelled. "I mean, Tessa!" Her heart pounded as she absorbed her friend's compromised position. Theresa was tied tightly to a chair, and Rosebud was looming over her like a vulture.

"Jo! Cay! Help!" Theresa's voice was desperate.

"What's going on here, Simon?" Victor asked Rosebud. His voice had lost its cool, slightly British accent. He sounded more like Al Capone or John Gotti.

Rosebud stiffened. "I've, uh, captured these two. They were trying to get away with the code, but I stopped them. I was going to call you as soon as . . . well, anyway, the situation is under control, Chief."

Chief?

Jo glanced at Caylin, who was staring intently at Victor. "Are you thinking what I'm thinking?" Jo asked.

"You're lying!" Victor screamed at Rosebud. "You were trying to pull a fast one on me, Simon. And I don't appreciate that." He crossed the room and put his hands around Rosebud's neck. "That code and all that it stands for is *mine!*"

Caylin grabbed Jo's arm. "Yes," she finally answered. "I'm thinking *exactly* what you're thinking." She paused. "It's definitely time for plan C . . . or D . . . or F!"

Victor pulled a gun from his pocket and pointed it at Rosebud's head. "You're not getting out of here with that code, Simon. And you're not going to see a dime of the cash I've got coming to me."

"Chief, I swear I was only trying to—"

"You're going to die tonight, Simon," Victor continued, his voice calm once again. "I had always planned to kill you—I just hadn't realized it was going to happen at this particular juncture. But so be it. We can't plan for all of life's little surprises."

Theresa gasped as the awful truth unfolded before her. Victor had been using her as a pawn all along. And he had used Rosebud, too. While Rosebud had thought he was going to outsmart Victor and get away with the code and the cash, Victor had planned from the start to do away with Rosebud when the time was right. Victor was the one who was trying to take control of the code—the executives at FutureWorks had nothing to do with it. Theresa wasn't going to shed any tears for Rosebud, but Victor's actions infuriated her.

"You're a traitor," she said quietly. "You're evil."

"And you're in deep, deep trouble, honey. Each and every one of you is going to die tonight," Victor said, waving the gun at Caylin and Jo. "One by one, you're all going to die!" Then slowly, methodically, he pointed the gun at Rosebud. "Then again, maybe I'll just put my tattooed friend in ICU. I think I can depend upon him to point the police in your direction."

Bang!

Rosebud moaned, grabbed his shoulder, and sank to the floor in a pool of blood.

Do something! Theresa silently urged her fellow Spy Girls—and herself. She struggled against her restraints, accidentally knocking over her chair in the process. As she fell, the all-important disk flew out of her waistband and landed at Victor's feet.

"Just as I suspected." Victor bent over to pick up the disk.

From her position on the floor Theresa watched as Caylin retreated several steps down the hall. Where was she going?

"Prepare to die, girls and guy." Victor slid the disk in his back pocket. "I have what *I* came for."

Behind Victor's back, Caylin assumed a sprinter's starting position. Then she *flew.* With a warrior-princess scream Caylin leaped onto Victor's back and knocked him to the ground.

Victor reached back and pushed his palm against Caylin's jaw. Her head reared, but she kept him pinned.

Jo raced over to Theresa's side. She cut away the binding ropes with a comb that doubled as a switchblade.

"Brad!" Theresa yelled. "Free Brad!"

Jo sped to Brad's side. Theresa shook out her numb wrists and hopped on her sleeping feet to help Caylin. Too late. Victor knocked Caylin off him. In a split second Victor was on his feet, waving the gun again.

"Cay! Look out!" Theresa screamed.

Too late again.

Bang!

Theresa heard glass shatter down the corridor.

Whew. Close call.

"Watch out!" Jo yelled from behind. She held a desk chair over her head, swung it back to gather momentum, and hit . . . Brad. Jo hadn't realized the guy was standing right behind her. He slid to the floor, unconscious.

"Brad!" Theresa yelled. "Oh, jeez!"

"Oops!" Jo turned to survey the damage.

"Too bad," Victor exclaimed. "You girls are mine now. Time to—"

Caylin jumped up on a desk and leapfrogged toward the office's low ceiling. She grabbed an exposed pipe. In a blur she swung and kicked her feet out. Bull's-eye. Her platforms smacked the creep in the head.

"—die." Victor's eyes rolled back and he fell forward in a heap.

"Get the disk!" Caylin yelled, dropping to the floor.

Theresa pushed aside Victor's coat and swiped the disk from his back pocket. "Got it!"

Jo grabbed the gun from Victor's fist and slipped it into her waistband. "Let's get the you-know-what out of here! Victor is starting to groan!"

Theresa paused. "What about Brad?" He was still lying on the floor, breathing easily but unconscious.

"We've got to leave him here," Caylin said, her hand on Theresa's shoulder. "He'll be fine. Without his gun Victor is powerless."

Theresa cast one last, longing glance at Brad and followed Jo and Caylin toward the elevator bank. Doors opened. Doors shut. Someone pressed "lobby." And they were going down, out, and away from the whole ugly scene.

Jo pointed at the gun hidden under her shirt. "You don't think it was a mistake to take Victor's gun, do you?"

Theresa shook her head. "We had no choice. Brad's life was at stake."

Jo nodded. "Yeah, you're right. Besides, what else could go wrong at this point? I think we've made all the mistakes we're going to."

"As long as we can get out of Seattle tonight, everything will be fine," Caylin said. "We can't give the cops even twelve more hours to find us."

"Spy Girls unite!" Jo cheered. "Good-bye, Seattle!"

Back at headquarters Jo and Theresa paced as Caylin dialed and redialed Uncle Sam's number.

"It's no use," she said finally. "He disconnected our direct line to him." She threw down the phone and sighed deeply. "As far as Uncle Sam is concerned, we don't exist. The Tower receptionist pretended she didn't even know my *name!*"

"Danielle!" Jo shouted. "We've got to call Danielle before Uncle Sam gets to her and tells her not to have anything to do with us."

Caylin didn't need to look up Danielle's number. She had memorized it the *last* time the girls had called her frantic for help. Caylin couldn't even believe it had come to this: They had completed their mission and exposed a crooked agent, yet The Tower was freezing them out. What did it all mean? She hoped Danielle would explain it all. Unless she was freezing them out, too.

Jeez.

"While you all talk to Danielle, I'm going to transfer the code," Theresa told them. "We can save the information in my can of mousse—it's actually a minisupercomputer."

"Good idea," Jo said. "I doubt any thief, double agent, or psychopath would go out of their way to steal our hair-care products."

Caylin punched in the last digit of Danielle's phone number in Washington, D.C. When she answered, her "Hello?" was groggy. Correction—it was near comatose.

"It's us!" Caylin said urgently. "Danielle, we need your help in the worst way."

"Victor is a traitor," Jo interrupted. "He shot

Rosebud and tried to kill us. Well, he would have, except Caylin knocked him out first. Anyway, we're still wanted by the cops—you know, they've got out that APB on Caylin and me. And now Uncle Sam won't even talk to us! Can you believe that? And—"

"Slow down," Danielle interjected. "Take a deep breath and get ahold of yourself, Jo. You're scaring me."

"You've got to help us, Danielle," Caylin said, taking over. "We need to get out of this state *pronto*."

"I sympathize with you girls," Danielle said with a yawn. "I really do . . . but unfortunately there isn't time for me to get to Seattle and lend you a hand." She paused. "You're on your own."

Theresa emerged from her bedroom, wielding her now precious can of mousse in one hand. "You've *got* to help us, Danielle!" she cried. "If you have to, abuse your authority or something. Please." She held the can of mousse close to her chest. "Just do what it takes to get us out of Seattle with the code."

"You have the code?" Danielle asked, her voice disbelieving.

"*Yes!*" all three chorused.

"Why didn't you say so before?" Danielle replied.

"Because we need to get out of here, like, yesterday!" Caylin said impatiently. "We need cash, and we need a car," she demanded. She was sure that Uncle Sam had canceled their Tower credit cards, and there was no way they would make it out of Seattle by plane. The airport was probably crawling with Feds. "If you don't provide those items, we're not going to be held responsible for our actions."

Danielle sighed. "All right, give me half an hour. I'll have a car and a couple of thousand in cash waiting for you outside HQ."

"Thank you!" Jo cried. "Thank you!"

"As soon as we're somewhere relatively safe we'll get on a plane to D.C.," Caylin declared. "You've got to meet us at the airport there so we can give you the code. It has to be you, Danielle. Sam won't even speak to us."

"Let me know when you're arriving, and I'll be there," Danielle promised. "But you girls better be careful. If there's any more trouble, even *I* may not be able to help you."

Caylin felt tears threatening to spill as she stared at the speakerphone. How could The Tower doubt their skills or their loyalty? Everyone made mistakes. Why were they being shut out?

"Danielle, you know . . . we really are good girls," Caylin began. "Don't believe anything that anyone tells you about us . . . because it's just *so* not true."

"Just get me the flight information when you have it," Danielle said. "We'll talk then."

Caylin hung up the phone, then turned to her fellow Spy Girls. "We've got a half hour to destroy any and all evidence that we were here."

Exchanging not another word, each girl set herself to the grim task. They had thirty minutes to erase themselves from Seattle, and they were going to need every second. This was the race of their lives. And a race *for* their lives.

Jo felt as if she hadn't taken a shower in a week, but she felt satisfied that no police raid on headquarters would ever reveal privileged information about the Spy Girls or The Tower. They'd dismantled, smashed, deprogrammed, and torn down everything. They'd thrown all volatile paperwork into the Dumpster in the alley and burned it to cinders.

All that was left downstairs was a normal-looking CD store with an empty cash register. There had been some moral quibbling over raiding it, but in the end all it yielded was about sixty-seven dollars. "No one pays cash anymore," Caylin had griped.

Part of Jo wondered why they were bothering to look out for the interests of The Tower at all. Uncle Sam had turned his back on them, and yet here they were, busting their butts to protect the integrity of the agency.

We're working for a greater good, Jo reminded herself as she kept a vigil for the car that was supposedly arriving any minute. No matter how The Tower treated them, the facts remained the same. Jo was committed to saving the world from the kind of people who had gunned down her father when she was fourteen.

Through the window Jo saw a bright pair of headlights coming down the deserted block in front of HQ. "Let's go!" Jo yelled to Theresa and Caylin, who were throwing the last of their belongings into duffel bags. "The car is waiting!"

Theresa emerged from Jo's room. "I got most of your stuff . . . but we didn't have time to pack everything."

"Who cares?" Jo asked. "Right now I'm more worried about my life than my sundresses."

"Let's rock and roll!" Caylin shouted, entering the living room with two duffel bags slung over her shoulder. "The sooner we blow past Seattle city limits, the happier I'll be."

The girls fled the apartment without looking back. They clattered down the narrow metal staircase to the now decimated warehouse and raced through Seattle Sounds. When they hit fresh air, there was a collective sigh of relief.

A tall, dark, thin man—The Tower agent Danielle had promised them—stood next to a Cadillac sedan. In his hand was an envelope bursting with cash.

"I'll take that," Jo said, grabbing the envelope.

The agent balked. "As an agent of the United States government, I feel compelled to advise you to turn yourselves in. The Tower no longer recognizes you as an official entity. Once captured by police, you will have to go through the legal system on your own." He paused. "Make things easier for yourselves and give up now. The real truth will come out, one way or the other."

What? Give up? Get captured? Hope the truth will just eventually "come out" after Uncle Sam turned his back on them?

Never.

Jo pulled Victor's gun out of her waistband. "Forget it!" she shouted, waving the weapon in the agent's face. "We're innocent!"

"Yeah!" Theresa yelled. "We were just doing our *job.* If The Tower is going to let us down, fine. But we're not going to let ourselves be sitting ducks for blood-hungry coppers!"

Caylin sprinted to the driver's side of the Cadillac and hopped in. "Get in, Spy Girls!" she called. "We're going, going, *gone!*"

Holding The Tower agent at bay with Victor's handgun, Jo opened the passenger-side back door for Theresa, who dove inside. Jo followed, and Caylin revved the engine. A moment later they roared down the street.

"Yeehaw!" Jo yelled. "Free at last!"

California, here we come!" Jo sang Wednesday morning. "California dreamin'! Wish they all could be California girls! I mean, guys!"

Theresa rubbed her eyes and blinked at the bright sun rising in the clear blue sky. The side of her cheek was stuck to the Caddie's leather interior, and there was a sharp, shooting pain in her right thigh. Theresa shifted in the seat. The seat belt clasp had been digging into her leg all night.

"Where are we?" Theresa asked, stifling an enormous yawn.

"We just crossed the border into California," Jo informed her from the driver's seat. "We are now officially two states away from the source of our horrendous troubles."

On the other side of the backseat Caylin opened her eyes and wiped some drool off her chin. "Did I hear someone say, 'California'?"

"Yep." Jo honked the horn. "Whoopee!"

"I'm starved," Theresa announced. A moment later her stomach growled so loudly that Caylin and Jo burst into giggles. "I guess that frozen burrito circa four-thirty in the morning didn't fill me up."

"I, for one, could use about a dozen cups of coffee," Jo said. "Not only have I been driving most of the night, but I also think I got slightly addicted to caffeine during my gig at Mega Mocha."

Caylin pointed to a green sign on the side of the highway. "Next stop: Peculiar, California," she announced. "It sounds like the perfect place for three tired, hungry Spy Girls to grab a little breakfast action."

Jo guided the luxury sedan toward the Peculiar highway exit. She sped onto the ramp, then slowed the car as they reached a traffic light. "Which way?" she asked.

Theresa sat up straighter and glanced from left to right. "Let's go right," she said. "I see a sign for a place called Moody's Diner down the road."

Two minutes later Jo pulled into the parking lot of a small diner that appeared to be a converted gas station. The parking lot was full of dusty pickup trucks and ancient station wagons. "Looks like we'll be pretty safe here," Jo commented. "I don't think Bobby Jim and Billy Ray will be too interested in a couple of wanted Spy Girls."

"Yeah, we'll just do the hat, scarf, sunglasses thing," Caylin said. "It's all we've got on us, anyway. And if anyone thinks it's strange, we'll claim we're allergic to the sun."

The girls trooped into Moody's Diner and slid into a large booth next to the window. For a few minutes they stared at their menus with the kind of intense concentration that only three starving fugitives could muster.

"I think I'll have the Zip-a-dee-doo-da Breakfast Bagel," Caylin announced when a gum-snapping waitress arrived at the table. "And a side of fruit salad."

"Double chocolate pancakes, a side order of spicy hash browns, and a bottomless cup of coffee, please," Theresa told the waitress.

"Make that a bottomless *pitcher*, please," Jo requested. "And I would love to try the Northwest Mountain Sunshine Plate. I've always wanted to have bacon, sausage, *and* ham during the same meal." She pushed her menu aside and stretched as the waitress retreated.

Caylin did the same. "Wow. I actually feel semi-normal for the first time since I set tail in that white limo."

"No kidding," Theresa agreed, pausing as the waitress set down a pitcher of coffee and three cups. "I think I could happily spend the rest of my life in a computer-free environment. I've had hard drives and mainframes coming out my nostrils." She had even dreamed about the mission during her not-very-satisfying night of sleep—encoders, decoders, and endless strings of numbers, letters, and passwords had raced through her brain as she tried to escape from a maze filled with treacherous Tower agents. It gave her the willies just thinking about it.

"I think we can say with some certainty that the worst is behind us," Jo declared, pouring milk into her cup of coffee.

"Yep. By tomorrow night we'll turn over the code, get back in The Tower's good graces, and be cleared of any miscreant deeds," Caylin said.

"Happy days are here again, let's smile, smile. . . ." Theresa's voice trailed off as she caught sight of the TV set that was positioned at the end of the diner's counter.

Wonderful. Right next to a lemon meringue pie under glass was the nine-by-thirteen-inch black-and-white image of Caylin's graduation photo. Man, she was starting to *hate* TV.

"Wh-what?" Jo stammered. "What is it, T.?"

"Um, scratch what I just said," she announced. "Don't look now, but it looks like our bizarro girl gang has just gone national."

Ouch. Double ouch. Triple ouch. What next?

Jo slipped quietly out of the booth and took a seat next to Theresa. She actually wanted to see what new horror the newscaster was sharing with the American public.

"Here you go, girls," the waitress said. She slapped each girl's order down in front of her. "I hope your mouths are as big as your eyes 'cause you three ordered enough food for five lumberjacks." She turned toward the TV. "Hey, there's a story about those crazy teenagers!"

Jo slid into her seat. I am invisible, she told

herself. Caylin was invisible. They were all invisible. She stared at the TV through her eyelashes and held her breath.

"Turn it up, Charlie!" the waitress called to the cook. "I want to hear this."

Every head in the diner turned toward the small television set. "Police believe that the now infamous Terrorist Trio have fled Seattle," the newscaster announced. "Through a wiretap, detectives were able to recover a telephone conversation during which one of the female gang members demanded two thousand dollars in cash and a vehicle from an unidentified female."

As the incriminating phone call played, the station showed security cam footage of Caylin and Jo walking—then running—through Arcadia.

"Is it as bad as it sounds?" Caylin whispered.

Jo nodded. "Worse." Naturally, the police didn't happen to pick up the first part of Caylin's conversation with Danielle. There was no mention of Victor or the fact that they were being framed.

"We really are good girls," Caylin's voice blared over the TV. "Don't believe anything that anyone tells you about us . . . because it's just *so* not true."

"Please tell me that's all they have," Theresa whispered.

Jo couldn't tear her eyes away from the small television. The newscaster was back on the air, reporting that an eyewitness had informed detectives that one Theresa Hearth had stolen important, highly sensitive information from the mainframe at FutureWorks.

"What eyewitness?" Caylin demanded. "Who?" It was obviously killing her that she couldn't see the TV from where she sat. Jo glanced at Caylin and saw that a vein in the side of her forehead was throbbing.

"It's Victor!" Theresa hissed. "That jerk."

Jo watched Victor being interviewed by a local Seattle reporter. He was in elegant mode, eminently trustworthy in a gray pin-striped suit and bowler hat. The louse.

"Yes, the entire situation was *quite* alarming," Victor said. "Theresa Hearth held myself and another young man hostage while she and her accomplices stole a computer disk holding a virus that could end the entire world banking system." He stared innocently into the camera. "They have already killed one man, shot another, and put countless people in danger. Those girls *must* be stopped—by any means necessary."

The newscaster reappeared on-screen. Thank goodness. Jo didn't think she could look at Victor's treacherous face for one more second without yakking.

"Evidence confirms the eyewitness account of events," the anchorman announced. Flash to FutureWorks security footage, obviously taken inside the thirtieth-floor elevator bank. A shadowy Theresa held what was clearly a computer disk. Another clip followed. Uh-oh. This one featured Jo waving a gun and shouting. Not good.

"One male cohort who failed to escape from the scene of the crime is being held in custody," the newscaster reported over the footage. "However, he claims to know nothing of the events that transpired, only claiming that he is innocent."

"Poor Brad!" Theresa whispered. "I can't believe I got him into this mess."

"If anyone sees these three young women, please contact the FBI immediately," the newscaster finished. "Once again, they are considered armed and dangerous." The plastic-looking anchor paused. "Alarmingly, that hasn't stopped teenage girls all over the country from taking up the cause of this mysterious Terrorist Trio. Parents are concerned."

Jo, Caylin, and Theresa stared at one another over the plates of rapidly cooling breakfast. None of them had taken so much as a bite of their meals.

"We're a *cause?*" Caylin asked softly. "What does that *mean?*"

"I think I'd laugh if our butts weren't on the line," Jo whispered. "I mean, they're, like, analyzing us. Caylin is the ringleader. I'm the brawn. And Theresa is the brains."

"We're like a cartoon," Theresa agreed. "Or a bad afternoon sitcom."

"Whoa . . . check this out." Jo turned back to the television. A group of teenage girls were on the screen, all decked out in Spy Girl disguise makeovers. Red hair. Skunk hair. Butterfly tattoos. Sunglasses.

Scarves. The whole bit. The girls were also holding up signs for the news camera: It's Just *So* Not True.

"The Terrorist Trio, are, like, conspiracy victims," one of the girls, made up like Caylin, told a reporter. "The system is against us! Young women get *no* respect!"

Suddenly Caylin swiveled around to face the TV set. "You go, sister!" she burst out. "Right on!"

Jo cringed as every person in Moody's Diner turned to stare at their table. She slid lower in the booth and prayed that the fact that each of them was wearing a hat, a scarf, and sunglasses wouldn't arouse suspicion.

Fat chance.

"The Terrorist Trio allegedly escaped Seattle in a midnight blue Cadillac Seville," the newscaster reported. "They are believed to be heading south."

In unison, the diner patrons craned their necks to look through the restaurant's huge glass windows. Jo knew what they were looking for. And she knew what they were going to see.

"Let's get breakfast to go!" Jo hissed. The girls picked up their food—plates, napkins, silverware, and all—and tore out of the diner.

"We'll send you the money for our bill!" Theresa yelled to the waitress as they ran.

"Yeah," Caylin agreed. "From jail!"

An hour later the Spy Girls were doing sixty-five down the highway. "Still no sign of troopers," Theresa reported from her lookout in the backseat.

"We're almost there," Caylin said. "The turnoff for Pirate's Cove is only two miles away."

"I know we all said we wanted to spend some time at your parents' summer beach house," Jo said as the Caddie raced toward the exit. "But I was hoping our stay would be under different circumstances." She cruised onto the exit ramp and followed Caylin's directions to the house.

"All we have to do is ditch the car and get in touch with Danielle," Theresa said. "Then we'll be outta there. Caylin's parents never need to know we stopped by without a formal invitation."

"Turn here!" Caylin instructed Jo. "The house is just a mile down the . . ." Her mouth dropped open. The usually deserted beach road wasn't deserted at all. First she saw the local channel nine news van. Then she saw the host of *American Investigator* sipping a cup of coffee. Then she noticed about a dozen cop cars.

"Curses! Foiled again!" Jo yelled. She slammed on the brakes. The Cadillac fishtailed as Jo did a one-eighty.

"Make a sharp left!" Caylin ordered. "I know a secret way back to the highway."

Jo drove the car onto a road that was little more than a trail, hoping for the best. In the distance she heard the unwelcome sound of sirens. "I hope you know what we're doing!" she told Caylin.

"I'll get us out of this," Caylin promised. "And then I'll take us to a place where I *know* we'll be safe."

"Where's that?" Theresa asked.

Caylin sighed. "It's a long story. I'll tell you on the way."

"Here we are," Caylin announced forty-five minutes later. "Mount Lassen."

Theresa was gazing out the car window and nibbling on a cold double-chocolate pancake. "All I see are trees," she said. "Are you sure there's an actual *house* here somewhere?"

"Take a right, Jo," Caylin instructed. She turned to look at Theresa. "Not just *any* house, *Tessa*. A mansion."

As Jo made the turn the woods opened up, revealing a huge log cabin built near the side of a mountain. A wide driveway led to what looked like a four-car garage. She whistled. "Your ex-sweetie lives well," Jo commented.

"Mike Takeshi isn't just an ex-boyfriend," Caylin said sharply. "He was my first love." Just seeing the oversize cabin caused a flood of memories. Caylin's first kiss. Mike carving their initials in the cellar wall. Picnicking in the moonlight. It all seemed as if it had happened a lifetime ago.

"Park here," Caylin instructed. "We can walk up to the house and make sure nobody is around."

"What makes you think no one is going to be there?" Theresa asked. She had polished off one pancake and moved on to another.

"The Takeshis are *never* here," she said. "Mike always flew out a couple of times a year to make sure the pipes weren't frozen or anything. But other than that, the place sat empty all through high school." She paused, staring at the house. "Except for one time . . . when a bunch of us came out for a vacation."

Jo threw the car into park, and the girls climbed out. "I hope there are a lot of canned goods in the cupboards," she said as they crept up the driveway. "I'm still hungry."

The girls neared the house and tiptoed to the windows at the front of the cabin. "Ssh!" Caylin ordered. "I'll make sure the coast is clear."

Jo and Theresa followed, giggling as they began to circle the property. Caylin heard a large branch snap behind her, then a loud "Ummph!"

She spun around. Jo had tripped over a fallen branch and landed face first. "Owwww!" she moaned, holding her ankle with both hands.

"Who's there?" A deep, masculine voice emanated from somewhere near the front door. "Tell me who's there."

So much for ultimate privacy. "It's me, Mike," Caylin called.

"Pike!" Mike Takeshi emerged from the house, every bit as good-looking as she remembered. Tall, delectable, with a surfer's body, honey-tanned skin, and a poet's eyes, the sight of Mike had always made Caylin's heart race.

He walked toward Caylin, paused, and enfolded her silently in his arms. She inhaled the scent of him, savoring the sensation of his strong arms around her waist. At last he pulled way. "Are you okay?" he asked. "I've been watching the news. . . ."

Caylin nodded. "We're fine—so far." She glanced over his shoulder. "Are your parents here?"

"Nope. They're in Europe for the month." He paused. "Is it true?" Mike asked Caylin, his brown eyes questioning.

Caylin raised her eyebrows. "Got a couple of days?" she asked.

Mike took Caylin's hand and led them toward the house. "For you, Pike, I've got all the time in the world."

I don't think I've ever fully appreciated the comfort of a leather recliner before." Theresa tipped back in the recliner and pulled out the footrest. "I could sleep for hours in this thing."

"Speak for yourself," Jo said. "I'm hoping Mike is going to offer me one of the many guest rooms this house has got goin' on." She gave him her most pleading, pretty-please look.

Mike grinned. "After the story you guys told me, I'll offer you a medal. You guys have been through hell."

"You believe us?" Theresa asked. At this point she was so used to being suspected of horrible crimes that she half wondered if Mike was going to pull out a gun and haul them off to prison.

Mike stared meaningfully at Caylin. "Pike has never lied to me. I would never doubt anything she said."

Theresa and Jo raised their eyebrows. The affection in Mike's eyes was hard to miss. Hmmm. Caylin had apparently neglected to fill in her fellow Spy Girls on some of the juicier parts of her past.

"You can't tell *anyone* what I've told you." Caylin scooted closer to Mike on a comfy plaid flannel sofa. "Not now. Not ever. This is, like, as top secret as top secret gets."

"Don't worry." Mike reached over to push Caylin's bangs out of her eyes. "I won't tell a soul."

"If you do, we'll have to kill you," Jo warned. An awkward silence followed. Jo laughed nervously. "Okay, *not* the time to joke about murder and mayhem. Understood."

"Remember when we took the snowmobiles up the mountain during our junior year?" Mike asked Caylin. "You buried yours in a snowbank and it took me four hours to dig the thing out."

Caylin laughed. "Excuse *me.* I'm not the one who practically set the whole house on fire because I didn't know I had to open the flue in the fireplace."

Theresa looked from Mike to Caylin, appreciating the warmth of their relationship. Maybe she and Brad would have the chance to form that kind of rapport . . . if she were still in Seattle and he weren't stuck in the clinker.

"You know what you need?" Mike began. "You need a good, old-fashioned four-wheeling adventure. It'll take your mind off this mess."

"I don't know. . . ." Caylin clearly wanted to go, but she looked hesitantly at Jo and Theresa. "Don't you guys think we should try to get in touch with Danielle?"

Jo shrugged, yawning. "I'm not doing *anything*

until I've had a serious nap. Go have fun. We'll hold down the fort—or the cabin, as the case may be."

Caylin grinned. She looked happier than she had in days. "All right!" She pulled Mike off the sofa. "But *I'm* driving."

"You're pretty cute as a redhead," Mike said as he climbed into the Hummer parked in the garage. "I think I could get used to the new you."

Caylin's heart fluttered as she slammed the driver's side door shut. All of a sudden she realized just how alone she and Mike were. The souped-up army vehicle was its own private world, and Mount Lassen felt as if it were a thousand miles away from civilization.

"You look great, too, Mike. You always do." She stared into his warm brown eyes, seeing years worth of good times reflected in their depths.

"When you broke up with me, you said it was because you needed space to find yourself," Mike said quietly. "But now that I know what you've been doing the past few months—or part of it, anyway—I have to wonder if you really wanted things to end. You know, between us."

Caylin swallowed painfully. "Don't make me answer that question, Mike. I can't."

He placed his hands on her shoulders. "You were trying to protect me, weren't you?" he asked. "Admit it, Caylin. You still love me."

"We were planning to go four-wheeling," Caylin

said, her voice high and shrill. "Don't get all heavy on me now."

Mike sighed as he relaxed into the passenger seat and buckled his seat belt. "I'll let this go for now, Pike. But I deserve some answers."

Caylin threw the Hummer in reverse and backed out of the garage. She knew she was due for a serious talk with Mike at some point. But right now all she wanted to do was climb high in the mountains and drive her troubles away.

"Are you asleep, T.?" Jo asked. They had staked claim on two twin beds in one of the Takeshis' opulent guest rooms.

"No," Theresa answered, rolling over in bed. "I can't stop trying to figure out how everything on this mission went so haywire."

"Same here." Jo nestled more deeply into the down comforter and contemplated counting sheep. Or llamas. Or anything that might help her get a few hours of much needed REM.

"One good thing has come out of this whole thing," Theresa commented. "Mike and Caylin are reunited."

Jo yawned. "Yeah . . . Caylin is lucky. Mike's a hottie."

"No kidding. The guy makes Brad Pitt look like chump change."

"I'm the only one who hasn't got any lovin' on this mission," Jo said, feeling cranky. "It's not fair." She had seen hot guy after hot guy waltz into Mega

Mocha, but she had kept her hormones under control in order to complete the mission without unnecessary complications of the masculine sort. What a mistake!

Theresa groaned. "Please! You got action on the last two missions. And might I add that your judgment regarding the male half of the species isn't always the best?"

"Okay, time to change the subject." Sure, Jo had kissed a few bad guys. What agent worth her weight in designer duds hadn't?

"Fine. Let's talk about our next move," Theresa suggested. "We're both obsessing over it, anyway."

Theresa was right. There was no time like the present to map out a plan. Goodness knew they needed one. "We can't go to D.C.," Jo concluded. "The cops might have heard us telling Danielle we would meet her there."

"We'll have to tell Danielle to meet us somewhere else," Theresa concurred. "But where?"

Jo thought for a moment. They needed anonymity, and they needed freedom of movement. Yes, that was it. The Spy Girls needed the ability to get lost in a crowd. They had learned from their Moody's Diner experience that taking the backwoods route wasn't a stellar tactic. "We'll go to Los Angeles," Jo said finally.

Theresa's eyes drifted shut. "Ah . . . L.A. Sand, beaches, sunshine. I like it."

Jo felt her own eyelids grow heavy. "Yeah . . . as

soon as Caylin gets back we'll make the call. Tonight. Tonight we'll head south."

"And after this is all over we'll make sure Brad is okay, right?" Theresa asked, mumbling almost incoherently.

"Right," Jo murmured. She floated into sleep, knowing she would dream of herself in the arms of a buff, tan lifeguard. Maybe finding romance on this mission wasn't totally out of the question after all.

"I'm going to take that tree trunk!" Caylin shouted to Mike. "I want to see what this baby is made of!"

"Go for it," Mike told her. "The Hummer knows no limits."

Caylin pressed the pedal to the metal and flew over a large, sawed-off trunk. She hadn't felt so relaxed in ages. With Mike she could almost forget that she was an international spy who had been disowned by her superiors. Unfortunately forgetting that a significant part of the American population wanted to see her hang wasn't so easy.

"Yes!" Mike yelled as they continued to speed up the mountain. "You haven't lost your touch."

The wind whipped Caylin's hair around her eyes and filled her lungs with fresh mountain air. I will prevail, she told herself. Correction. *They* would prevail.

"*Whooo . . . eee!*"

Suddenly Mike frowned. "What's that?" he asked.

Caylin glanced at him. "What's what?"

"That noise!" Mike twisted in his seat and gazed out the back of the Hummer. "Hey, someone is following us!"

Caylin gripped the steering wheel.

No. No way.

She peered into the rearview mirror, and her heart sank. Someone was gaining on them. She saw a tall, lanky figure astride a Harley-Davidson chopper, tearing up the mountain road. Victor! There was no way. How could he possibly have tracked them to Mike's house? Unless . . . unless someone had tipped him off?

"That's Victor," Caylin told Mike. "In case you don't already know that particular fact."

"How would *I* know?" Mike asked.

Caylin sped up the Hummer, shaking her head. "Never mind. Just stay down. Victor doesn't joke around." She would find out soon enough whether or not Mike had betrayed her. Maybe he had been lying all along when he had said that he believed their story. Maybe he thought she was a crazy murderer and that Victor was a good guy fighting for justice. Please, don't let that be the case, she pleaded silently. Caylin couldn't stand the thought of Mike doubting her.

"He's gaining!" Mike shouted. "We've got to do something!"

Caylin breathed a sigh of relief. Mike sounded sincere. "What? Tell me what to do!"

Mike ran his fingers through his thick, dark

hair. "We've got to immobilize him. It's the only way we'll get away. That chopper can probably go a hundred and ten miles an hour."

Mike was right. At this point outrunning Victor wasn't possible. This road led straight to the top of the mountain, where Victor would have every opportunity to aim for her head. There was only one way back down the mountain, and it involved her turning around and retracing their progress. She would have to face Victor and win.

Caylin slammed on the brakes, reversed, and turned around. And then she headed straight toward the enemy. As they got closer to the motorcycle Caylin saw that Victor was steering the powerful bike with one hand. In the other he held yet another gun. This one looked bigger and more powerful than the last.

"Mike! Get out and run!" Caylin shouted. "If you bail now, you can make it back to the cabin safely."

"No way!" Mike shouted. "I'm not going to leave you alone with that psycho! I'll die first."

Despite the present circumstances Caylin smiled. Mike was with her. He was on her side, and he was going to help. Her faith in humankind restored, she started to formulate an insane, dangerous plan. "Do you have a rope?" she asked.

Mike unbuckled his seat belt and dove into the back of the Hummer. "I've got a bungee cord. Will that work?"

Caylin nodded. "Yep . . . now take the wheel." In

a maneuver that she would have laughed out loud at if she had seen it in a Bruce Willis flick, Mike and Caylin switched places with the Hummer in motion. With Mike driving, Caylin was free to concentrate on bringing Victor down.

They met Victor head-on. He spun the motorcycle around, sped alongside the Hummer, and prepared to shoot. The terrain was bumpy, and he obviously was having trouble taking aim. But Caylin wasn't going to give him a chance to get off a shot. No way.

Caylin wrapped the bungee cord around her wrist and took a deep breath. She had one chance to bring down Victor. If she blew it, they would all die. She had no doubt that Victor would spare no one. The man was a cold-blooded killer.

Caylin threw back her arm and unleashed the bungee. The cord sprang out just as she had planned and wrapped itself around Victor's wrist. Caylin clenched every muscle in her body and held on tight. "Yes!" Caylin shouted.

Victor's face paled as he lost control of the motorcycle. The gun flew out of his hand, landing somewhere in the woods. A moment later Caylin was able to pull him off the chopper with the strength of the cord. He landed in a pile of brush . . . moving but groaning.

Mike hit the brakes and jumped out of the Hummer. "What are you doing?" Caylin yelled.

"I'm going to kill that guy!" he shouted.

Caylin leaped out of the Hummer and followed

Mike into the woods. He was standing over Victor, wielding a large branch. "Got any questions for this dude, Pike?" Mike asked.

"Don't kill me," Victor whimpered. "Please, don't kill me."

"How did you find us?" Caylin yelled at Victor. She had to know. If he answered, maybe she would let him live. Maybe.

Victor groaned. "I traced your car," he grunted. "The agent who brought you the Caddie was in on this with me the whole time!"

Jerk. Idiot. "I should take you out right now," Caylin muttered.

Victor stared at her. "But you won't . . . will you?" he asked. "You girls are too pure to kill anyone on purpose."

He was right, darn it. Caylin didn't want blood on her hands—or on Mike's. "Don't test me," she said, anyway, hoping she sounded tougher than she felt.

"You can't escape me—not even if you murder me," Victor said. "You never had a chance. I've got contacts *everywhere!*"

"Can I do the deed?" Mike asked, waving the branch.

"No way." She paused for a moment. "But can you help me tie him up instead?"

Mike dropped the branch. A few short moments later Victor had been effectively hog-tied with the bungee cord.

"See if your 'contacts' can help you get out of *this* mess, dude," Mike taunted. He jogged toward the motorcycle, lifted the chopper upright, and rolled it toward the Hummer. "We're taking this with us. If you ever work your way out of those knots, we'll *all* be long gone."

Caylin felt her eyes brimming with tears. Mike had come through for her. She had needed him, and he had been there. The guy deserved to know the truth—it was the least she could offer. She ran to help him with the chopper.

"You know, Mike . . . you're right," Caylin said softly as she guided the bike toward the Hummer. "I didn't really want to break up with you. I never stopped caring."

Mike didn't respond. He began to lift the chopper. Caylin immediately got behind him and pressed her hands against his warm back to spot him. With one final grunt Mike managed to get the motorcycle into the back of the Hummer. He wiped sweat from his brow.

"Mike . . . did you hear what I said before?"

"Yeah," he replied, his eyes glued to the ground. "But you still need your space, right?"

Caylin didn't answer. She got in the driver's seat and revved up the engine. "Maybe someday."

Mike hopped into the front seat, put his hands on either side of Caylin's face, and planted a firm kiss on her lips. "Yeah . . . maybe someday."

With that promise in her heart, Caylin sped toward the giant log cabin. Victor was incapacitated, but he wasn't out of the game. Once again it was time for the Spy Girls to hit the road running.

The Spy Girls lingered with Mike in the small parking lot of the Motel 6, where they had spent the afternoon and evening hiding out and giving one another brand-new makeovers. Mike had proved himself to be an invaluable ally, having sacrificed his male ego in order to clean off the shelves at Rite-Aid of any and all beauty products that caught his eye. He was also providing the Spy Girls with another getaway car—this one a bright red Cherokee Jeep. It was the ultimate SUV.

"Do you have everything?" Mike asked. "Wet suits? Lotion? Surfboards? Self-tanner?"

"Check, check, check, and check," Jo answered. "Once we don our surfer babe gear and descend upon Venice Beach, no one will guess that the so-called Terrorist Trio is walking among them."

"Thanks again, Mike," Theresa said, giving him a hug. "Without you Caylin might have been dead right now—not to mention Jo and me."

He laughed. "Hey, the last eighteen hours have been the most exciting of my life. I should be thanking you three."

Jo stepped forward and gave Mike a loud smack on the cheek. "You're an awesome guy, Takeshi—we'll get the Jeep back to you when the madness dies down."

He shrugged. "No prob. Take your time."

Now that the easy good-byes were over, Caylin glanced significantly from Jo to Theresa.

"We'll just, uh, go ahead and get in the Jeep," Theresa said.

As her fellow Spy Girls climbed into their latest getaway car, Caylin took Mike's hands in hers. "Thank you for . . . everything. Especially for believing in me. I'll never forget it."

Mike hugged her close. "Thank *you* for telling me the truth. Now that I know why we had to break up, I don't feel like the biggest loser on the planet." He leaned back and wrapped a strand of Caylin's now black hair around one of his fingers. "You were beautiful as a blond and adorable as a redhead . . . now you're sultry as a black-haired raven."

"Bye, Mike," Caylin whispered.

"Be safe, Pike." He let go of her hair, turned, and retreated toward the anonymous motel room. The plan was in motion now. Later, when the Spy Girls had been on the highway for a few hours, Mike would drive the Hummer to the house of a friend in Carmel, California. There he would lay low until the Spy Girls were able to prove Victor's treachery to The Tower.

Caylin hopped into the backseat of the SUV

and buckled her seat belt. "Let's hit it!" she told Jo. Part of her wanted to wallow in sweet memories of the past, but she knew that getting wrapped up in some nostalgia trip would distract her from the task at hand—namely, the Big Handover.

"On the road again, I juuust caan't wait to get on the rooad again!" Jo sang from behind the wheel. "Next stop, Los Angeles, Califor-nye-yay!"

Dawn was breaking as the girls closed in on the City of Angels. Jo, Theresa, and Caylin were wide awake, trying in vain to map out the exact steps that would get them out of their mess of the week.

"So you guys talked to Danielle?" Caylin asked.

"Yes, for the third time," Jo answered. "We called her secret cell phone number. She agreed to get on a plane to Los Angeles. We're supposed to call again to establish a meeting place."

"When do we call?" Caylin asked. She was chewing on a piece of her now black hair, staring into the lightening sky.

"Whenever," Theresa answered. "Danielle's probably eating an early bird breakfast special as we speak."

Jo tossed Theresa the cell phone Mike had insisted they use during the last leg of their mission. "Reach out and touch someone," she told her fellow Spy Girl. "The sooner we know exactly where we're going, the faster we can make this whole episode a thing of the past."

"Do you think we'll have jobs once this mission

is over?" Caylin wondered. "I mean, Uncle Sam is going to forgive us for those screwups, right?"

Theresa shrugged. She had been pondering the same question as they sped through a long, dark night on the freeway. A week ago Theresa wouldn't have believed that The Tower could so easily lose faith in their loyal Spy Girls. But according to Jo and Caylin, Uncle Sam had been unrelenting on the telephone. Jeez. The guy had refused to take their calls for the last twenty-four hours! But maybe there was still hope. Maybe.

"If worse comes to worst, we can pool our limited resources and open up a private investigator agency," Jo commented dryly. "We can chase down stolen pets and deadbeat dads."

"Sounds thrilling," Theresa responded. "I can use my high-tech computer skills to flip through dusty files in some small town city hall basement."

"Just go ahead and make the call to Danielle," Caylin said. "I'm not willing to give up on The Tower yet. We've been through too much to call it quits."

Theresa dialed Danielle's secret cell phone number. The phone rang four times before Danielle finally picked up. When she spoke, her voice was almost drowned out in a sea of static. "Hello!" Danielle shouted.

"It's us. The Terrorist Trio." Theresa didn't think any further identification was necessary.

"I can't talk long," Danielle said. "There are . . . things happening here."

"Things? What things?" Things were bad. Things meant more trouble for the Spy Girls. Theresa could hear that much in Danielle's voice.

"Sam knows you all got in touch with me," Danielle informed Theresa darkly. "And he's not happy. This whole incident has put The Tower in a very awkward position."

"What are you saying, Danielle?" Theresa knew her voice was laced with a combination of panic, anger, and desperation, but she couldn't help it.

"The drop-off will be tricky," Danielle said. "We'll still meet in Venice Beach, but not in a cafe as we discussed—it's too risky."

"Where?" Theresa asked. "Just tell us where, and we'll be there."

The static on Danielle's end of the line was so heavy that Theresa could barely hear her. "Meet me in three hours at lifeguard stand number . . ." *Ssshhhh.* The static grew even louder.

"What? I didn't hear you!" Theresa yelled into the cell phone. "Which lifeguard stand?"

Click. The line was dead. "Dang," Theresa growled. She cut the connection, then immediately dialed Danielle's cell phone number again.

"The mobile unit you have called is not responding or is outside the coverage area. Please try your call again later." The computerized voice on the other end of the line repeated the message one more time. Then there was nothing but a dial tone.

"Well?" Caylin demanded. "What's the deal?"

Theresa bit her lip. Danielle hadn't sounded like herself—not at all. "I don't know. But I think we had better be prepared for the worst."

"What else is new?" Jo quipped, maneuvering the Jeep onto the Pacific Coast Highway. "Los Angeles—ready or not, here we come."

The temperature had risen to a balmy eighty degrees when Jo turned the SUV into an all-day, five-dollar flat fee, public parking lot on Pacific Avenue and Venice Boulevard.

"Man. I dreamed about spending a day at the beach when we were freezing our butts off in Prague," Jo said, switching off the engine. "But I had pictured myself in a tiny bikini, lying on a blanket, with a trashy romance in my hand and a cooler of diet Cokes at my side."

At least they were dressed for the locale. The girls had stopped at a gas station in Malibu and changed into their ultimate surfer girl wear. Now they looked like *Baywatch* extras.

"I know what you mean," Theresa agreed. "This wet suit is wedgy city."

Jo pulled out a tube of neon pink zinc oxide and slathered her nose. "If all goes well, maybe we can spend the afternoon relaxing in the shade of some hot lifeguard."

"I'm worried about Mike," Caylin stated for the umpteenth time.

"He called the cell phone when you were paying for the last tank of gas," Jo reminded her reassuringly.

"He's safely ensconced in Carmel, probably riding a tasty wave at this very moment." She, too, had been glad to receive Mike's phone call. Between him and Brad, the Spy Girls had managed to jeopardize the lives of two possible love interests. So much for danger being the great aphrodisiac.

The girls climbed out of the Jeep, taking only what was absolutely essential—surfboards, sunglasses, a backpack holding the all-important mousse can and a few miscellaneous spy gadgets, and Mike's cell phone. They were silent as they traipsed across the parking lot and headed to Venice Beach, each girl lost in her own flood of tension and anxiety.

"Wow," Jo exclaimed when they reached the boardwalk. "This place is *packed*." There were people everywhere. Vendors had already set up shop along the boardwalk, selling everything from temporary tattoos to used clothes to five-minute massages. A psychic sat on a small crate, her tarot cards shuffled and ready for a customer. And there appeared to be about a thousand lifeguard stands. Danielle could be *anywhere*.

"What now?" Caylin asked, surveying the sea of people.

"We start looking," Theresa said. "And we don't stop until we find Danielle."

"We also keep an eye out for any and all suspicious persons," Jo said. "Victor could be here . . . or any number of his evil accomplices."

"Trust no one," Caylin said. "That's our motto."

The girls jogged down the beach, stopping at

each lifeguard stand to search for Danielle. There were a lot of hot lifeguards but no sign of the tall woman whom they had come to think of as their guardian angel.

Finally out of breath, the girls collapsed in the sand. "Yep, this is a real day at the beach," Theresa said. "This is my idea of re-lax-ation." She carefully inspected her arms and legs. "I think I'm getting a sunburn."

Jo pointed to a group of idle sunbathers who were lazing nearby on a huge beach blanket, listening to their transistor radios. "Listen up, girls. Those folks are tuned in to the news, and I don't think the news is good."

"Reports indicate that the Terrorist Trio have descended upon Venice Beach," the announcer read. "Undercover police have saturated the area. They have informed KFI radio that they are determined to catch the renegade girls by day's end. In other news . . ."

Caylin groaned. "Great. Just what we need. Undercover cops." She glanced over her shoulder. "Hey, is that guy looking at us?"

Jo and Theresa stared at a man standing nearby. He was dressed in surfer gear, but his skin was suspiciously pale. The guy looked like he hadn't been on a beach in years.

"Scatter!" Jo ordered. "Reconvene when it's safe at that lemonade stand over there."

"Check!" Caylin and Theresa chorused.

Jo sprinted up the beach, losing herself in a

crowd of volleyball players. "We need a server!" someone shouted. Jo took this as a sign and grabbed the ball.

As she slammed it over the net she saw none other than Pale Man saunter past. He headed onto the boardwalk and disappeared into a burger joint. Her work here was done. She aced one more serve and tossed the ball to the girl next to her. "Your turn!"

Caylin bobbed in the ocean, waiting for the right wave to come along. Jo and Theresa might not like their wet suits, but hers felt like a second skin. She had known immediately how she was going to disappear. The waves were like home to her.

A perfect wave rolled toward her, and Caylin stood on her board. Seconds later she was riding toward shore with the sun on her back and the wind in her hair.

Heaven.

She hit the shore and saw Jo strolling toward the designated lemonade stand. Caylin jumped off her surfboard, tucked it under her arm, and jogged off to join her fellow Spy Girl. Missions came before tasty waves, unfortunately.

Theresa walked up to Jacie's Lemonade Stand and took a seat next to Jo and Caylin, who were sharing a jumbo frozen.

"What happened to *you?*" Caylin squealed.

Theresa glanced at her arms. "I had to *blend,*" she exclaimed. She had spent the last twenty minutes getting a henna tattoo from a woman with a pierced chin.

Jo giggled. "You look like something out of *The Guinness Book of World Records.*"

"Enough joking around," Caylin said. "Let's resume the search."

They got up, pitched the lemonade, and headed down the beach. At last Theresa saw a familiar head of shiny dark hair in the distance. "Danielle!" she said excitedly. "There's Danielle!"

"Of *course,*" Jo said. "She's standing next to lifeguard stand number *three.*"

"We should have guessed," Caylin agreed, picking up the pace and running toward the stand.

As the girls neared the lifeguard stand Theresa felt as if the mousse can was burning a hole in her backpack. More than anything else in the world she wanted to deposit the code safely into Danielle's capable hands.

"Where is she *going?*" Jo shrieked.

Uh-oh. Danielle was walking toward a pier next to a tall, thin man wearing an oh-so-out-of-place long trench coat.

Theresa stopped in her tracks. "You don't think Danielle is in on this with Victor, do you?" she asked.

"She's been acting awfully strange . . . ," Jo offered. "Maybe . . . maybe she's betrayed us. No. No, she wouldn't do that. Would she?"

"The Tower agent who delivered the Cadillac and the money to us in Seattle was in cahoots with Victor," Caylin reminded them. "And Danielle was the one who sent the guy to us in the first place."

The girls stared at one another silently. The tension was so thick that it could have been cut with the proverbial knife.

"No," Theresa said finally. "Danielle would never turn on us."

"Never," Jo agreed immediately.

"No way. No how." Caylin's voice was firm, unwavering.

"Which means . . . that Victor is after her," Theresa concluded. "He's going to kill her and then come after us for the code!"

"Ohmigod! We've got to save her!" Caylin cried.

The girls jogged toward the pier, hot on Danielle's trail. Two hundred yards away she hopped—or was pushed?—into a speedboat docked near the pier.

"If we go after her, the cops are going to notice," Theresa pointed out. "We'll be sitting ducks!"

"There's no other option," Jo yelled, sprinting toward the pier. "We've got to do this for Danielle . . . and for The Tower."

Nodding in mutual agreement, the Spy Girls raced toward the pier. Do or die. Do or die.

This threat again, also delivered [illegible] did the money [illegible] [illegible] [illegible] [illegible] the [illegible] [illegible]

The [illegible] [illegible] that [illegible] over was so thick that it could have [illegible] [illegible].

"No," [illegible] said finally. "[illegible]"

"[illegible] immediately."

"[illegible]"

"[illegible]."

"[illegible] that [illegible] [illegible]"

[illegible]

[illegible]

[illegible]

[illegible]

[illegible]

Sorry, dude," Caylin said to a Teva-and-swim trunks-clad guy who was about to hit the water on a Jet Ski. "Duty calls." She gave the guy a well-placed shove and jumped onto the Jet Ski. Beside her Jo and Theresa did the same to two other unsuspecting beach dudes.

"Rock on!" Jo yelled, revving up her engine. "Pacific Ocean, watch out!"

Each of the girls unleashed her Jet Ski from the pier and raced out to sea. The speedboat was gaining distance. Every moment counted.

Caylin was aware of nothing but pounding waves as she sped toward the boat. Come on, Danielle, she urged silently. Hang in there. Help was on its way.

Suddenly Jo zoomed up beside her, pointing toward the shore. Several large men were each climbing onto a black-and-white Jet Ski. Cops!

"Hurry!" Jo mouthed, taking the lead.

The girls skipped over wave after wave, closing in on the renegade speedboat. Behind them the Venice Jet Ski cops were in hot pursuit. Suddenly the air was filled with even more noise. Caylin glanced up and saw a helicopter hovering over the speedboat.

Oh no! Danielle, in the arms of Victor, was being hauled up to the helicopter via a swinging rope ladder. Caylin saw the distinct glint of a gray metal gun shining in the sun.

No time to lose. The girls pulled up beside the now empty, idling speedboat. One by one each ditched her Jet Ski and climbed aboard.

"What do we do?" Jo yelled over the helicopter's roar. The copter still hovered above the boat.

Caylin caught the swinging rope ladder and held on with all of her strength. "We've got to go up there!"

"Victor had a gun!" Theresa screamed. "He could kill us all!"

"But if we *don't* go, he'll *definitely* shoot Danielle!" Jo shouted.

Theresa nodded. "We're goin' up."

Caylin climbed up the rope ladder, struggling to contain the overwhelming terror that gripped her. Each rung seemed a mile away as her muscles ached with the effort of climbing.

Up above, two large male hands shook the ladder back and forth. Caylin glanced down and saw that Jo and Theresa were still dangling beneath her, still holding on for dear life. But the ocean below was falling away. The copter was going up!

"Can you make it?" she screamed to her partners.

Jo's face was bright red, Theresa's sickly white. Agony was etched in their pained expressions.

"Yeeahh," Jo groaned.

Theresa managed a nod. Nothing else.

Caylin continued to pull herself up the ladder. She focused on the bottom of the helicopter, forcing herself to forget the huge, roiling ocean that lay thousands of feet below her.

Higher. The helicopter was moving steadily into the sky, making this mad journey more dangerous by the second. Rung by rung, Caylin approached her destination.

"Just *go!*" Jo screamed, her words almost lost in the wind. "*Go!*"

At last Caylin reached the door of the helicopter. She could see Danielle sitting inside on a built-in seat. The agent didn't appear to have been harmed. Which was the first good sign Caylin had seen in what felt like forever.

"Danielle." It was the only thing she could utter.

She hoisted herself up and searched wildly for Victor. Where was he? Flying the helicopter up front?

Jo appeared next. "Man . . ." She heaved herself up next to Caylin, panting. They crouched on the small floor of the craft, wedged behind the pilot's seat.

"You're not going to get away with this, Victor!" Jo yelled, regaining her breath. "I don't care if I have to rot in jail during a nine-month trial! You will *not* succeed!" She glanced around the tiny helicopter.

"Where is he?" she asked Danielle.

Before The Tower agent could respond, Theresa's head popped up. "The code," she moaned. "I've got the code."

Caylin and Jo grabbed her arms and pulled her over the edge. "You made it, T. You made it." But the helicopter was still ascending. The strong pair of hands that had been shaking the ladder moments ago could appear at any moment to push all of them out the open door.

"Where's Victor?" Theresa panted.

"Just give me the code!" Danielle shouted.

Caylin nodded to Theresa to go ahead. They were beyond the point of no return. To distrust Danielle at this point was unthinkable.

Theresa pulled off her backpack and stuck her hand inside. Finally she handed Danielle the can of mousse. Their fate was in her hands. Or Victor's. Or some other unknown person's who she was too tired to think about.

Danielle looked at the object in her hand. "I know I don't look my best," she said. "But am I really having *that* bad a hair day?"

The girls stared at Danielle in wonder. They were in a life-and-death situation, and she was making jokes!

"We have to subdue Victor!" Jo shouted. "We're all going to die."

Danielle laughed. "Victor isn't here, Jo. He's in jail." She gestured toward a tall, thin guy who was lounging in the corner of the copter seat. "Meet

Frank Grant. He's a good friend of mine . . . and a Tower agent."

"What?" Caylin shouted. "You mean he was the one who kidnapped you and was holding you hostage?"

Danielle laughed again. "Congratulations, Spy Girls! You've passed quite a test!" She was beaming, her eyes brimming with tears. "My Spy Girls, the heroines."

In the roiling water below the helicopter a dozen Jet Ski riding cops flashed the girls the thumbs-up sign. Their cheers were audible even over the roar of the copter blades.

"Those aren't real cops," Danielle explained. "At least not the kind you're thinking of. The Tower hired them to pursue you this morning." She paused. "And I knew Frank resembled Vince—aka Victor. He was a stand-in."

"Will someone *please* explain what's going on?" Theresa demanded.

"You were right about Vince," Danielle said as the pilot of the helicopter headed toward shore. "The Tower had suspected all along that he was working against us, but we had no way to know for sure without involving you three. Testing him was part of your mission."

She paused. "Initially Vince's plan wasn't to kill you, Theresa. After taking his position at FutureWorks he'd made a deal with Simon Gilbert—Rosebud, as you call him—for a percentage of the profits from the code. But Vince and Simon had a big falling-out, and

Vince knew that Simon was planning to take back possession of his code."

Theresa swallowed. "But where do I fit in here?"

"Victor thought that by enlisting you to extract the code, he'd turn you against The Tower," Danielle explained. "He figured you'd help him in the technical department in exchange for a few multibillions. But along the way Rosebud got clued in as to your arrival and had planned to kidnap *you* so that *you* could do the dirty work for *him.* And from that moment on, everything went haywire."

"So both Rosebud and Victor were trying to use me in order to backstab the other." Theresa shook her head. "Weird."

"Where's the V-man now?" Caylin asked.

"The Tower caught up with him at the base of Mount Lassen. He's in custody." Danielle grinned again. "One more bad guy in the slammer."

"So Uncle Sam *knew* the V-man was bad the whole time?" Jo shrieked. "Why didn't he tell us?"

"It was imperative that Vince not suspect that you suspected *him* from the outset," Danielle explained. "We had to trust that you would figure out the truth."

"I don't understand," Theresa said. "Why didn't Uncle Sam tell us that once the mission went awry? I mean, he totally cut us off from The Tower like we were common criminals."

Danielle smiled. "Once the ball started rolling, Sam decided that the circumstances provided a perfect means to test all of your abilities. We wanted to know that you would come out of the mission on top without the backup support of The Tower—and you did!" Danielle leaned forward and patted each of the Spy Girls on the back. "You all put your heads together, achieved your mission, and remained loyal to The Tower under the most difficult circumstances. Bravo!"

"Talk about a close call," Jo murmured. "I didn't think we were going to make it."

"I was starting to consider enrolling in court reporter's school," Theresa agreed.

Caylin laughed. "I wasn't worried—not at all!"

The girls giggled with relief. They had really and truly proved themselves worthy of the Spy Girls name. Whew!

On Friday afternoon Jo, Caylin, and Theresa stood on the steps in front of the Santa Monica courthouse. Next to them, standing in front of a podium, was Officer Bascovitz. He had flown in from Seattle especially for the press conference that was currently under way.

"I am happy to announce that Jo, Caylin, and Theresa have been proven innocent," Officer Bascovitz boomed into the microphone. "The real killer has been caught and is now being held without bail."

"Thank goodness Brad was let out of prison," Theresa whispered to Jo and Caylin. "When I called him this morning, he said a date with me should come with a warning label." She giggled. "But he *also* said that if I was ever in Seattle again, I should look him up." She paused. "Do you think we'll be back in Seattle anytime soon?"

"No!" Jo and Caylin whispered in unison.

"The law enforcement agencies of Washington and California would like to issue an official apology to these girls," Officer Bascovitz continued, gesturing toward the Spy Girls. "They were the unwitting victims of a criminal conspiracy."

In the large audience of reporters and supporters cheers erupted. "We knew you were innocent!" one girl yelled. She waved her sign—Hail the *Terrific* Trio—in the air.

Off to the side, TV reporters were already filing their stories for the evening news. "Although it is not known yet how the police came to realize that the supposed Terrorist Trio were innocent, the facts today speak for themselves." A blond, perky reporter smiled into the remote cam in front of her. "We'll have more at eleven."

Officer Bascovitz turned to the girls. "Would you like to make a statement?" he asked. "After all of this sensational media coverage, the American people want to hear your stories."

Jo stepped up to the podium. "I would like to thank our loyal supporters," she said, grinning at all of the teenagers who were holding signs and cheering. "We were in the wrong place at the wrong time, and we hold no grudge against the Seattle police department." She paused, smiling into the crowd. "And to all of you cute guys out there, *yes*, I *am* single!"

Caylin rolled her eyes at Jo's last comment and approached the podium. "I have two things to say," she announced. "The first is this: Mom and Dad, your love and support means everything to me. The second thing won't mean anything to a lot of you, but it will mean a lot to the person who matters." She leaned close to the microphone. "Thank you, Mike." Caylin stepped away from the podium and nudged Theresa forward.

"We're all looking forward to resuming our everyday lives now that this huge mix-up is behind us," Theresa said brightly. "We're just three *normal* American teenage girls . . . living three *normal* lives." She joined Caylin and Jo, who had retreated from the podium.

"Three cheers for three great girls!" a voice boomed out from the back of the crowd. The girls looked at one another. That voice . . . it was familiar.

"You don't think?" Jo said.

They stared in the direction of the booming voice. There stood a shadowy figure. He was wearing a long coat, the upturned lapels hiding most of his face. A white derby hat had been pushed low on his head. The man turned his face in the direction of the Spy Girls and flashed a quick thumbs-up.

"Uncle Sam!" Theresa cried. "It's him!" Even as she spoke, he disappeared into the crowd. And then he was gone.

"We never even got a chance to thank him," Caylin joked.

The girls retreated to the other end of the steps as Officer Bascovitz took questions from reporters. Talk about an action-packed week! It was going to take them a month of soap operas and bonbons to recover.

"Do you really think we're going to have to give autographs?" Jo wondered.

"We can't let down our adoring fans," Caylin pointed out.

"Dang! I wish I had practiced my signature." Theresa giggled.

Suddenly an eager face appeared before them. The young woman's short, dark hair was mussed, and she wore a fashionable sundress. In one hand she carried a Leave the Girls Alone! sign. Danielle in disguise!

"You guys are, like, my heroes," Danielle gushed in a singsong voice. "Can I, like, give you a present?"

"Why, yes, young fan, we would love a gift," Jo said, winking at Danielle.

Danielle placed a large snow globe in Jo's hand. Inside the crystal globe were miniature Swiss chalets and tiny porcelain skiers. As Danielle faded into the crowd of reporters the Spy Girls exchanged excited glances.

"Does this mean what I think it means?" Jo asked.

"Ladies, we're going to Switzerland!" Caylin

squealed. "So much for our nice, relaxing beach vacation."

"Alps, here we come!" Theresa exclaimed.

The girls hugged one another close. This mission had been accomplished. But another awaited them. After all, they had a whole world to save.

About the Author

Elizabeth Cage is a saucy pseudonym for a noted young adult writer. Her true identity and current whereabouts are classified.

Watch out, Swiss misses and misters—the Spy Girls are hitting the slopes! The disappearance of a hot young rock star has been linked to a bizarre international conspiracy—and the secret may be hiding in the remote, snow-covered mountains of Switzerland. Their base of operations, a glamorous ski resort, has Jo, Caylin, and Theresa so stoked they can barely keep their minds on their mission. Will all play and no work lead to a tragic end for the Spy Girls?

Ain't no stoppin' us now!
Get down and
boogie-oogie-oogie with
Spy Girl mission #4:

SPY GIRLS ARE FOREVER

Coming
March 1999